AF485825

Copyright © 2022 Kayla Isaac
Published by T'Ann Marie Presents, LLC
All rights reserved. No part of this book may be reproduced in any form without written consent of the publisher, except brief quotes used in reviews. This is a work of fiction. Any references or similarities to actual events, real people, living or dead, or to real locals are intended to give the novel a sense of reality. Any similarity in other names, characters, places, and incidents are entirely coincidental

Cold Outside: Ari Lennox

Here I Go: Kash Doll

Yoncé: Beyonce

Digits: Young Thug

Whatever You Like: T.I.

Super Gremlin: Kodak Black

Good Morning Gorgeous: Mary J Blige

You: Lloyd

Break of Dawn: Michael Jackson

Butterflies: Queen Naija

Sex Drive: Tiara Thomas

Stroke: IV4

Patience: Russ

Trey Songz: Can't Be Friends

Hate Our Love: Queen Naija and Big Sean

Rylee Artello

"Ms. Artello, I got a question," quizzed my seventh grade student, William, who had given me nothing but trouble the entire semester. This would have been my third time in a row teaching William, and I was convinced that he just loved being in my class at this point. I was a seventh grade teacher at Rising Star Middle School in Charleston, South Carolina.

"Yes, William?" I sighed, already having a feeling that foolishness was about to come out of his mouth.

"Can I come with you to Atlanta? I know this is your last day here, but I can't be stuck with no other teacher. I can hide in your suitcase; my mama won't care if I'm missing."

"William, you know you can't come with me to Atlanta," I laughed.

"William, she's right. What is this, your third time repeating her class? She's tired of seeing you. What about me, Ms. Artello? I ain't ever been to Atlanta; I wanna go," said my other student, Jazzy.

"I'm going to miss everybody as well, but I cannot take y'all to Atlanta with me. I'm sorry, guys; you all know it's been wonderful teaching all of you; it really has, but this will be the last day you all see me. I'm so sorry."

Seeing their sad little faces and hearing the groans coming from their mouths only warmed my heart. I had received multiple gifts from everyone in my class, along with gifts from staff members. One thing I knew for a fact was that I was going to leave an imprint on Rising Star Middle School. Teaching here for six years had been nothing but gleeful to me, but it was time for me to spread my wings for something bigger. I was now leaving Rising Star Middle School to start my journey as a professor at the University of Georgia. Thankfully, Spring Break officially started tomorrow, and I had a week break away from children. After the bell rang, I stood up, prepared to gather my things and go, but when I saw my students still sitting in their desks, I raised my eyebrows with perplexity written all over my face. Any other day, my students would've been rushing out the door as if their favorite celebrity was calling them. Now, they were just sitting there with those same sad looks on their faces. Not to mention my class was the last class period of the day, and I knew they were ready to go home and get their Spring Break started.

"This is the first time you guys have ever stayed in your seats this long after the bell rang," I laughed before crossing my arms.

"We don't want you to go," one of my students pouted.

"I'm going to always come back and visit. I promise, guys."

"Put it on yo' set you coming back to visit," said William.

"Boy, if you don't get out of my class."

"Say you put it on your set that you coming back, and I'll believe you."

"William, sweetheart, I promise I'm going to come back and visit. One thing about me that you all should know is when I make a promise, I stick to it. Just like I'm promising to come and visit, I need you all to make a promise to me that you will work hard and pass all of your classes. I don't want y'all to get to get eighth grade and act like ain't taught y'all nothing."

"We promise," they said in unison.

I received a hug from all of my students before they darted

out the door. As soon as the kids poured out of my class, my coworker, Shanice, came in with the same sad look on her face.

"Uh uh, don't come in here with that. You already had me on the phone for three hours last night, talking about how much you're going to miss me. I don't need another three hour rant on why I should stay. I have to meet with my parents for lunch."

"Well dang, I can't mourn the loss of my favorite coworker?"

"Mourn me? You act like I'm dead."

"It's going to be dead here without you."

"Like I told the kids, I'm going to come back and visit."

"You better. Now give me my hug before I chain you to the school and hold you hostage."

We shared a laugh before embracing one another into a hug. After grabbing my box of belongings, I made my way outside to my baby blue Lexus LC 500. Getting inside, I placed my box of belongings into the backseat, along with my Michael Kors bag. Cranking it up, I made my way towards California Dreaming to meet my parents for lunch. Ari Lennox's "Cold Outside" played throughout my car the entire drive there.

Brown skin honey, said won't you creep into my bedroom?

You lookin' real good now, tell me what it do

I heard you got a girl though, what's it got to do with me?

Oh, she don't have to know

I'll meet you, quarter to three

Spotting my mother's Porsche in the parking lot, I pulled next to it before getting out and heading inside. Spotting them sitting near the window, I rushed over before hugging both of them.

"About time you got here, I was about to order my food

without you," my father chuckled lightly.

"Y'all know I had to say goodbye to my students. They made it extra hard for me today."

"How do you feel about the opportunity in Georgia?" quizzed my mother.

"I feel great. I'm just going to miss my students."

"I know leaving is hard, but the pay is a lot better, and you'll get to know Drayton better. You know he's the dean," my mother wiggled her eyebrows at me, causing me to laugh.

Growing up, my mother and father had always paved the way for my little sister and me. My mother was a dental hygienist, and my father was a defense attorney. My sister, Remi, had already given my parents their first grandchild, but sadly, she chose the wrong man. He was a deadbeat, and my parents made it known every day that they didn't approve of her actions, but they still treated her like a princess since she was the youngest. My parents thought it was a great idea to set me up with someone they both approved of. I assumed they did this because they feared that I was going to end up like Remi. The thing was, I was thirty-two years old, and I had been in enough fucked up relationships to know when I was choosing the wrong man. My priority wasn't even on men right now. I just wanted to enjoy my career and live life freely. A relationship was the last thing on my mind. If a relationship did come to the surface, it would have caught me by surprise. My parents' issue was that they felt as if I was reaching up in age, and they wanted me to find the right man and give them grandkids. Usually, when parents tried to hook their children up with someone they found suitable, it didn't usually go well. But for me, I actually enjoyed the conversation Drayton and I had together. Although it was long distance due to him living in Georgia, I still enjoyed the company, even if it was virtual — that was, until he and my parents had a hell of a conversation that led to me being offered a job in Georgia.

"Oh lord, here you go," I laughed.

"He's a good man, isn't he?" asked my father.

"He's definitely a good man. Well, from the conversations we have. I can't speak fully on him when we haven't even met in person yet."

"Well now that you're going to Georgia, you'll be able to meet him in person. Are you excited?" my mother quizzed.

"Mama, I'm excited to start the job, not go down there to date."

"Mhm, if you say so. So, what are you doing for Spring Break? You going out of town again? I know you had fun in Greece last year by yourself, but we both know money is a little tight because of the move."

"Mama, I have a good bit of money to treat myself if I did decide to go out of town," I sighed.

"I don't care about you going out of town; I just feel like you should bring someone. Hey, maybe take your sister."

"I'm not taking Remi nowhere with me," I rolled my eyes.

I loved my sister, but sometimes she made me want to choke her ass out. Remi was twenty-one years old and acted like she was sixteen. She was immature at times, and if I was planning to treat myself during Spring Break, she damn sure wasn't coming with me. I planned on having fun, not babysitting.

"Why? She doesn't do anything but get on those old folks' nerves down in West Ashley. Take her with you, wherever you're going."

"I don't know daddy; I'll think about it. And this year, I'm staying in state."

"Where are you going?"

"To Myrtle Beach."

"Why Myrtle Beach?"

"It'll be a minute before I can come back home after I get settled in Georgia. I'd rather go out with a bang in Myrtle Beach."

"Go out with a bang with your sister. There's no way you sitting in Myrtle Beach by yourself. You call that having fun?"

"Who said I was going by myself?"

"Who's going with you?" asked my mother.

"Porsha," I replied. My parents looked at me like I had grown two heads.

My friend, Porsha, was definitely a wild card. She was born and raised in New Orleans, and one thing she did was talk shit and back it up. Porsha and I had met a long time ago when my parents took my sister and I to New Orleans over Spring Break. She was the crazy to my cool, and even though our friendship was long distance, we talked every day and treated each other like we lived next door.

"Porsha? Porsha, as in that wild ass girl from New Orleans? She's driving all the way to South Carolina?" my mother quizzed as if she didn't believe what was coming out of my mouth.

"Stop it, mama. Porsha isn't that bad."

"Don't she got a child? Why is she coming to Myrtle Beach with you? You really feel like having her loud ass son in your ear while the both of you are trying to have fun?"

"Uh uh, don't do that. First of all, her cousin is watching her son while she's gone, and secondly, we are going to have fun regardless. You act like Remi don't have a whole child herself, and you want her to come with me," I scoffed.

"I just want you and your sister to spend some time together.

Is that too much to ask?"

"It's not too much to ask, but you act like Remi is bearable when she's not."

"I'm just saying, Remi, come on she's your sister, give her a chance.." my mother retorted.

"So am I. Just think on it."

"Well, I leave in two days."

"Two days is enough time to think."

I already knew the rest of the conversation was going to consist of my parents begging me to let Remi accompany me on my trip. After lunch was over with my parents, I went straight home to continue packing my bags for Myrtle Beach.

"Bitch, I swear I'm gonna get some dick when I touch down in South Cackalackin!" Porsha squealed on the phone.

"It's South Carolina and stop it. Didn't your ass have a baby already? You shouldn't be worried about dick."

"Your problem is, you need to be worried about dick, with your uptight ass."

"Oh my God, here you go," I sighed.

"Oh, I know what it is. I know what your ass is worried about. You worried about that Mr. Dean of Georgia's dick."

"Get off my phone; you're cutting up already."

"When is it not like me to cut up?"

"I have something I wanna run by you, though."

"Wassup?"

"How do you feel about Remi coming with us?"

"Oh, hell nah!" she yelled.

"I knew you were going to say that."

"If you knew then why ask? You know I already owe your sister an ass whippin'."

"My parents want her to come."

"Does this look like Chuck E. Motherfucking Cheese to you? I don't like that hoe, and you know that. Your sister just does something to me. You know I don't like her."

"Well, you're probably going to have to suck it up if she does come. I don't have time to sit here and argue with the both of you the whole time."

"Yeah, yeah, yeah. Tell the little bitch to keep her stupid ass comments to herself."

Just from the way Porsha was going in on the phone, I already knew things weren't going to be how I wanted it to be.

Cree "Trigg" Wright

"You talk to your daddy yet?" asked my mother.

"Nah, not yet," I sighed, pinching the bridge of my nose.

"That figures. I don't even know why I bother, I can't—"

My mother's sentence was cut short by an erupt of coughs. Rushing to her aid, I looked at her with a look of concern. My mother was in the late stages of breast cancer, and seeing her like this had broken me down to the core. Breast cancer ran in my family, and it was the same silent, but deadly, weapon that took my grandmother away from me. My mom should have been in the hospital. Shit, that was where I was more comfortable with her being. I knew her time was coming, and she knew the same thing. That was part of the reason she didn't want to be admitted to the hospital. She didn't wanna be confined to a bed, hooked up to machines, waiting for God to take her home.

"Ma, you can't keep getting yourself worked up like this," I sighed.

"Worked up? Cree, baby, I'm fine."

"You're not fine, and we both know you're not fine. I already told you that you could come and stay with me."

"I'm not moving in with you. Shit, you practically done moved back here, if you want me to be honest. Your big behind been squeezed up in that twin size bed every night."

"I just be wanting to make sure you're good."

"That's not what it is."

"It is that."

"Cree, you've been practically living here since Kimmy died," she replied, referring to my younger sister.

Just hearing my sister's name turned my entire mood sour. Clearing my throat, I then tugged at my chin hair.

"I just worry about you sometimes, ma."

"I worry about you more, Cree," she retorted, putting her hands on my cheeks.

"You have nothing to worry about; I'm straight."

"I have a lot to worry about. You're my baby boy; I worry all the time. You're worrying about my cancer, and I'm worrying about your wellbeing. Baby, ever since Kimmy died, you've changed."

"Can we not talk about her right now?"

"You don't even say her name."

"Ma, please," I pleaded. She sighed before shaking her head and taking a seat.

"Fine, I'll leave it alone for now."

"Thank you."

"Thank you my behind. I said I'm leaving it alone for now. I'm serious about what I said earlier."

"What part?"

"Everything, but mainly being worried about your wellbeing."

"My wellbeing?"

"Cree, baby, you're in this house, looking after me almost

every day. You have the same routine. You go to work then get off work, just to come back here and take care of me."

"What's wrong with that?"

"A lot is wrong with that, baby. I don't wanna feel like you stopped your life for me."

"Stopped my life?"

"You know exactly what I mean. You're twenty-three years old, working in your uncle's tattoo shop. I know you don't wanna do that your whole life."

"I'm not doing that my whole life."

"I just want better for you, Cree."

"Better like what?"

"I want you to go back to school, get a better job — live for you, baby."

"I—"

"Stop trying to argue and just listen. Look, I know Spring Break is literally right around the corner."

"What about it?"

"I did something that I feel you deserve."

"And what's that?"

"I planned a trip for you and your friends to go to Myrtle Beach for a week."

"Myrtle Beach? A Week? Ma, I'm not leaving you for a week, especially if I'm going to be three hours away. What if something happe —"

"Nothing is going to happen; I'm going to be fine."

"Where did you get money to plan a trip for me anyway?" I

raised my eyebrow at her.

"You must have forgotten that the Marine Corps paid your mama good," she laughed lightly.

"You got a point, but still, I'm not going."

"The hell you are. Boy, you know how much I paid for that damn hotel room, how much money I done put in an account for you to enjoy yourself? You about to make me whip your ass," she gave me a stern look.

"What if I bring you with me?"

"Cree, no. Look, if you wanna make me happy, and I mean really make me happy, go on this trip and enjoy yourself. If you don't do it for yourself, do it for me."

"Who's gonna look after you?"

"Do I look like a got damn dog to you? A fucking goldfish? Cree, I can take care of myself."

My mother and I stared each other down before I threw my hands up in surrender, already knowing I wasn't about to win this debate. She smiled and stood up before planting a kiss on my cheek.

"I get on your ass because I love you, you know that."

"I know."

Before she could respond, there was pounding on the front door, and I already knew who it was.

"Tell that dyke ass friend of yours I'm gone beat her ass if she keeps knocking on my damn door like the police."

I let out a loud laugh before rushing to the front door and opening it, revealing my best friend, KC. She walked in before dapping me up. When she locked eyes with my mother, she held an apologetic look on her face.

"Hey, Ms. Wright," she smiled.

"Hello, Katherine."

"Come on now, Ms. Wright, I thought we talked about this."

"I don't care what we talked about. Your mama named you Katherine, so that's what I'm calling you. I been calling you Katherine since you came out of the womb. I don't know who the hell KC is."

I waved for KC to follow me outside before my mama finished tearing her a new ass hole. One thing my mother was always going to do was speak her mind, and she didn't give a damn who you were. KC and I took a seat on the front porch. I watched as she pulled out a freshly rolled blunt before running it under her nose and smiling.

"You better not be smoking that shit on my front porch, Katherine!" my mother yelled from inside.

"Damn, yo' mama got K9 senses now? I ain't even light it."

"That shit strong; she probably smelled it when you walked in," I laughed.

"She gone quit calling me Katherine. I done told her that's not my name."

"You know she don't care about that shit," I laughed.

"Yeah, yeah, yeah. What you been up to, though?"

"Same old shit. You went and situated that problem I told you about?" I asked.

"You know I did. Lil' nigga went out like a lil' bitch. Bet you his ass would think twice before disrespecting the set."

"Good. As bad as I hate making examples out of motherfuckers, it had to be done."

"You already know how it is. Red Haven every motherfucking day and night, baby. Rep that shit proudly," she replied, flexing, showing her tattoo on her bicep that repped our set.

KC and I had been tight since the third grade. She and I had been through so much shit, you would have thought we were blood. But blood never made family; it was the connection and bond you had with a motherfucker that truly made you blood. Growing up in Charlotte was no easy journey for either of us. Since I was a military brat, I stayed with my grandmother while my mom was off at sea. My pops was an international aid worker, so I rarely saw him. I believed that my parents' marriage didn't last because they never saw each other. The only true thing they had in common was me and my sister, and that's what kept them going strong — that was, until I got older, and I could see through all the bullshit. They knew I saw through it. Once my sister, Kimmy, was killed, my parents split right after the funeral. Shit had a nigga traumatized. My mom was too torn up about losing my grandmother and my sister, she neglected me in a sense, and my pops just vanished. He moved to Georgia and said the hell with everything — including me.

The difference between a regular deadbeat ass father compared to mine was that he admitted to being just that and tried to fix shit right away. But still, the love and care that I needed as a teenager didn't keep me out the streets. When I turned sixteen, I met KC's big brother, Kojo, for the first time. . Kojo had been big trouble in the streets for years. He was the leader of the Red Haven, one of the most infamous gangs here in Charlotte. No matter what part of Charlotte you were in, you heard about Red Haven. He was trying to recruit my ass just off meeting me for the first time. I had common sense enough to tell him no because my grandmother didn't play that shit. On my seventeenth birthday, all that shit went out the window. I lost my grandmother on that day, and after that, I had a lot of built up anger that I needed to unleash. I was Kojo's right hand man and so was KC. Sadly, Kojo lost his life in a shootout against another nigga who was trying to make a name for himself. Neither one of them made it.

That same night, Kojo made me promise him that I would take over Red Haven, a promise that I wasted no time agreeing to keep. Since that day, KC, my boy Bozz, and I had been running shit and making sure shit ran smoothly. Unlike them other trouble making ass gangsters who ran the streets, I made sure me and my boys stayed out of trouble. When you thought of a regular ass gang, you instantly thought of shootouts and a bunch of bullshit behind it, but Red Haven was different. Yeah, we shook the city at times, but it was only when needed. We helped our city more than we destroyed it. That was a big change from what Kojo was doing. But just like Kojo, I had to be on the lookout for hating ass motherfuckers. One thing about me for sure was that I knew I had real ass niggas on my team watching my back. Even though KC was a woman, she was a hard, cold nigga, and she looked like one too. She wasn't like those weird ass studs who were confused about their look. She knew for a fact she was that nigga. KC stood at six foot one and kept a low cut. She was far from anything nice to play with on any level.

"Wassup with your mom, though? She getting better?"

"I wish I could say she was," I sighed.

"You know I'm always here, right?"

"I know."

"Good. She's like my second mama too."

"But there is a problem, though."

"What's the problem?"

"She planned a trip."

"A trip where? And that's good, right? She don't get out the house much."

"She planned a trip for me."

"Oh shit? Aight, Ms. Wright, I see you. Where we going?" she smiled, rubbing her hands together and licking her lips.

"Myrtle Beach."

"Oh shit! I'm down for that!" she exclaimed, getting excited.

"I bet you are. I'm not comfortable with that, though."

"Why not?"

"I just don't wanna leave her by herself, especially for a week. That's too long."

"Calm yo' ass down, nigga. Ms. Wright is a strong ass woman. She been going this long."

"That's the point. She been going this long. What if I'm gone, and she can't go any longer? What if I'm not here?"

"Stop talking about what if and talk about now. Your mom is a strong woman, and she can handle herself. Her ass was a sergeant in the Marines. She got this shit."

"I hope so."

"I know so, nigga. This Myrtle Beach. We ain't ever been to no damn Myrtle Beach. I'm ready to see all the ass and titties I can see."

"That's all your ass stay worried about," I laughed.

"Oh, I forgot. You can't worry about ass and titties because Olivia pussy juices done baptized you like holy water."

"You know I don't fuck with Olivia no more. Cut that bullshit."

"Yeah right. I know I'm gonna fuck you up if you don't take this free trip your mama planned. Shit, nobody got time for your basic ass to be hesitating on shit."

"I'm not leaving until I make sure she straight, though, and that's on the set."

"As you should; that's your mom. If it makes you feel any better, I can get my mom to check on her sometimes."

"Ms. Brown be working graveyard shifts. I don't wanna bother your mom."

"You're not bothering her. Look, anything to get your mind at ease. Your mom wouldn't have booked this trip if she felt like you didn't deserve a break and she couldn't take care of herself."

"I know."

"Then act like you know, nigga. When was the last time you talked to your pops, though?"

"A few days ago. You know shit be short and sweet when it comes to him."

"What that fool talking about?"

"He ain't talking about shit. Just the same old, same old."

"I bet so."

"Where Bozz at, though? Y'all usually pull up together."

"You know Bozz fat ass had to get something to eat on the way here. Nigga eat more than Tammy from My 600-lb Life. Bitch ass gone text me talkin' about, "Oh KC, you gotta try Chicken King's new wings. Them bitches bust." I bet they do bust, just like his ass bustin' out the seams of them tight ass True Religion jeans he be wearing. Fat fucka," KC spat.

"Damn, you mad, ain't you?" I laughed.

"Yeah, I'm mad. I left my food in that nigga car the other day and his bitch ass gone lie and say he didn't see it. Like nigga, I know you ate my shit."

"You still trippin' over that shit?!" Bozz yelled, walking up.

Bozz was a bit on the heavy side, and he stood at five six with freckles on his face. I met Bozz my eighth grade year of middle school. He had moved from France after his parents split. I knew he was good ass people when he came swinging full force when some punk ass niggas tried to jump me in the bathroom. Bozz and I had been tight ever since, and he proved his loyalty damn near daily.

"You know I'm trippin', nigga. I been hungry as hell, and you knew my mama wasn't cooking shit."

"That shit hit too," he laughed.

"You know what else gone hit? When I run you over with your mama beat up ass Bentley."

I laughed and shook my head, watching my best friends go at each other's throats. All I could do was think about how I was going to make it through a week in Myrtle Beach with this goofy ass nigga. How I was going to have fun with my mom on my mind was another.

Rylee Artello

"Bathing suit, check. Toothbrush, check. Toothpaste, check," I stood back, looking at my suitcase.

"Condoms, check! My rose, check! Three grams, check!" said Porsha, walking into my bedroom.

I shook my head at her antics. Porsha had shown up at my spot at six in the morning and ever since, she'd been wide awake and on my ass like white on rice. Her excitement was very evident. All I wanted to do was sleep since I was the one driving, and all she wanted to do was run her damn mouth. I loved Porsha, but she talked entirely too much.

"Really?" I said with my hands on my hips.

"Yes, I just gotta make sure I have everything."

"Porsha, babe. If you did forget anything, it's back in New Orleans," I laughed.

"Ok so, I could always buy something if I forgot it. I know I'm tired as hell, I'll tell you that. Baby, that eleven-hour drive from Nola make you wanna beat a bitch down."

"I told you to catch a flight."

"Nah, I'd rather feel like beating a bitch down after an eleven-hour drive. And I know exactly what bitch is gonna catch these hands when I see her."

"Don't start, Porsha."

"What? I been wanting to whip your sister's ass since day one. I hope you know she not coming with us, right."

"She is coming."

"What?"

"I got tired of hearing my parents' mouths, and then, she started calling and begging to come, so I couldn't say no."

"You could have said no. Fuck your parents and your sister. They can suck my clit through a straw."

"Porsha, chill with all that."

"Chill with all what? You know how I feel about your sister."

"Can you promise me something?"

"You know I don't do Christian-like things. I don't make promises because I know for a damn fact that I'm going to break them. You want somebody to make a promise to you, you better go to one of them old ass dirty pastors in the church who be using the church money to buy booty. One thing they know how to do is make a promise and sometimes keep it. But with me, I ain't keeping no promise."

"Porsha, I'm serious. If we're going to be together for a week, I need you and Remi to not act an ass when we get there. My middle schoolers behave better than y'all."

"Mhm, whatever. I'll try. That lil' rat-faced bitch got one thing to say to me that I don't like, and I'm gone beat her ass. Matter fact, she bet not breathe on me. Hoe better not even speak to me. That's it, that's that."

"First of all, we're going to be in Myrtle Beach for a week. You can't go a whole week without talking to each other."

"Bullshit. I bet you I can."

"Porsha," I warned.

"Don't Porsha me. I don't wanna hear that shit."

"Can you please make this a good trip? Not only for you but for me. You know I have to go to Georgia and start fresh down there. I wanna enjoy my break."

She looked at me with crossed arms before letting out a dramatic sigh. She ran her hands down her face before throwing her hands up in surrender.

"Fine, I'll leave the hoe alone."

"Thank you."

"Yeah, yeah, yeah, whatever. What you got to eat in this bitch? I'm hungry. My damn spine and my back fucking like two anorexic bitches."

"You better get some cereal; we jump on the road in literally three hours."

"I don't want no cereal. A damn po boy sound good as hell right now. Ooh girl, especially with a cold drink. Parkway got the best motherfucking po boys in Nawlins." I laughed just hearing her Nola accent break through.

"Well, sorry to break it to you, baby, but ain't no Parkway here."

"Duh, I know this. Anyway, let's talk about that nonexistent sex life of yours," she wiggled her eyebrows.

"Nonexistent? What makes you think it's nonexistent?"

"Because whenever you get a nigga or you getting some dick, you run to me and give me the juice. I ain't heard no juice in a minute. Let me find out that pussy drier than the Sahara."

"Worry about your own pussy, stupid."

"Mhm, but for real. Any new men in the picture? You still talking to homeboy in Georgia?"

"I am, actually," I smiled.

"Ohh, you smiling like the motherfucking Grinch, spill it."

"There's nothing to spill. He's just very cool people. I love his vibe and everything about him. He's respectful and—"

"Blah, blah, blah, blah. Fuck the respect part. You need a nigga that's gone disrespect the body and respect the mind and soul. When was the last time you had that pussy punished?"

"Porsha, really?"

"Don't tell me you ain't had none since Darnell triflin' toxic ass."

"Fuck Darnell. I'm not worried about him. After him, I took it as a learning lesson. Never trust a nigga who gone play the victim and gaslight you."

"Facts. His ass better be lucky I was in Nawlins, because he would've gotten this work."

I laughed and shook my head at how crazy Porsha was acting. Darnel was my ex-boyfriend who I thought I was going to marry. One thing I could say about myself was that I would never fuck a friend again. That friends with benefits bullshit wasn't all it was cut out to be. Darnell worked a lot, and I respected that — that was, until I caught him cheating on me with his so-called stepsister. Walking in on that was like some Lifetime movie shit. I put my all into that relationship, and it truly broke me down to the core. From that point on, I made focusing on myself my main priority.

After making sure I had everything packed, Porsha and I placed our suitcases in my car so that we didn't have to worry about it later. I took a quick shower before throwing on a plain white crop top tee, blue ripped denim jeans, and a pair of rhinestone Steve Madden sandals that showcased my freshly painted white toes. Staring into my full body mirror, I flipped my thirty-inch, bone straight bundles over my shoulder, as I admired the way my fit hugged my curves. Growing up, I was always on the curvier side. I stood at five foot three at two hundred and forty-five pounds. One thing I wasn't afraid to do was flaunt my curves. I was all about body positivity, and on this trip, I was prepared to show all of Myrtle Beach everything I had.

"You got everything?" I asked Porsha.

"Nope."

Before I could ask her what she forgot, the sound of my sister's Jeep pulling in my yard cut me short. "Here I Go" by Kash Doll blasted through her speakers as I opened the door, leaned on the frame, and watched her get out. She was dressed in a white, sheer jumpsuit with a black thong, and her nipple rings were on full display. The straight bundles she usually kept in her hair were replaced with a red lace front wig that was styled in a bob. All I could do was shake my head at how she was dressed. She left nothing to the imagination.

"You got to be fucking kidding me," Porsha mumbled with a raised eyebrow.

"I have to agree on what you're thinking."

"Hey, big sister!" she exclaimed, walking up to me with open arms. She pulled me into a hug before planting a kiss on my forehead. Remi was an inch and half taller than me, sharing the same almond brown skin color. She smiled big and wide, showing off her braces. Remi was thick but not as thick as I was.

"Where the hell are your clothes?"

"What are you talking about?" she asked, clueless.

"You look like you about to clock in at somebody's strip club."

"More like working somebody's corner," Porsha mumbled.

"I know you not talking. Look at what you got on," Remi

snapped at Porsha.

I looked at Porsha's fit and then back at Remi before sucking my teeth at her. Porsha had on jean shorts that were evidently riding up her ass, showing her toned cheeks and a blue bralette crop top. She looked like a hoochie, but she didn't look as bad as Remi.

"Remi, you can see your fucking titties. Go change," I pointed to the inside of my house. She had clothes here because she often came over to stay a few nights whenever she felt like getting on my nerves.

"Come on, Rylee, there's nothing wrong wit—"

"You're not coming behind me like that. You know when I say something, I stand on that."

She looked as if she wanted to test my gangster but decided against it. She stormed into my house before shortly coming out in a yellow sundress that complemented her skin. Once she placed her suitcase in my trunk, I wasted no time in jumping on the road.

"So where are we staying? I heard The Captain Quarters is the best hotel there. Plus, the view is amazing," said Remi.

"We're not staying in a hotel."

"Where we staying?"

"In an Airbnb. When I planned this trip, I originally invited two of my coworkers and Porsha. So, I got us a nice, big ass vacation home. You know when Spring Break hit, everybody's trying to get into a hotel. When I was booking, all the good hotels were already filled. So, I luckily found a good deal on this Airbnb."

"Well damn, I'm sorry for crashing your trip," Remi scoffed.

"You didn't crash my tri—"

"Don't lie to that damn girl. She know she crashed our damn trip."

"Bitch—"

"Uh uh, I done gave the both of you the talk. Don't start."

"Fine. But how many rooms are in this vacation home?"

"Six."

"Six? Damn, and there're only three of us? Why so many rooms?" Porsha quizzed.

"That was all they had," I sighed.

"Well, how would y'all feel if I tell you that it's not going to be three of us?"

"What are you talking about, Remi?" I asked, looking at her in the rearview.

"I've been wanting to tell you this, but you've been so busy with trying to move and get your shit together."

"What did you do?"

"You have to promise me that you won't get mad."

"Oh hell nah, bitch, stop the car. Tell her what I told you. Only Christians and pastors make promises, bitch!" said Porsha, turning around to look at Remi like she wanted to fight for me. One thing I hated was last minute surprises, and Remi knew that.

"You know I love you right, big sis?" she smiled.

"Remi, what did you do? Please don't tell me you did some stupid shit."

"I invited Darnell."

When she said my ex's name, I slammed on the brakes so hard, she flew up front and hit her head on the radio.

"Ah, fuck! What the hell, Rylee?!" she screamed, sitting up, rubbing her temple.

"What the fuck, Remi?! Are you serious?! You can't be serious!" I was fuming. Why the hell was she in contact with my ex after everything he'd done to me? Just from hearing that bullshit, I wanted Porsha to whip her ass just this once.

"His sister died and—"

"The sister that he was fucking? Good, I hope she died choking on dick," I snapped.

"Rylee, stop, can you listen, please?"

"What?" I huffed.

"Me and Darnell talk now."

"The fuck you mean, you and Darnell talk?!" Porsha yelled, asking the same question I was going to ask.

"I'm talking to my sister, not you."

"Bitch, shut up. You fucking your sister's ex? I'm surprised she ain't put your ass out on 95."

"We only started talking after the both of you broke up. If you don't feel any type of way about him anymore, why does it matter if me and him are talking?"

"It matters because you're her fucking sister, and that's triflin'. Why hop on a dick your sister already had? You a dirty hoe!" Porsha spat.

"I'm not gone be too many more hoes and bitches. Rylee, get your Pitbull before I put her down."

"How about the both of you shut the fuck up! Look, I planned this trip to clear my head and have fun, and I'll be damned if I let the both of you ruin it. Porsha, please leave her the fuck alone. And Remi, don't say shit else to me the entire drive. I don't give a fuck if you and that man get married tomorrow, just leave me out of it."

The car went silent before I turned my radio up. One thing I didn't play about was my peace, and if it came to it, I would pay to stay in one of those crusty ass roach motels in Myrtle Beach and still have the best time of my life. No one was going to ruin my Spring Break for me, not even Darnell's dusty dick ass. "Yoncé" by Beyoncé blasted through my car to kill the awkward silence.

"I sneezed on the beat and the beat got sicker," I sang low.

"Yoncé all on his mouth like liquor," Porsha sang, nudging my shoulder, making a stupid face. As bad as I didn't wanna crack a smile, I couldn't help but to.

"Yoncé all on his mouth like liquor," Remi wiggled her shoulders and sang.

I guess they knew they fucked up because one thing they had in common was trying to make me smile when they angered me. We sang loud and ratchet to the song and the many songs that played on the long playlist I made for the trip.

When we arrived in Myrtle Beach, my jaw dropped in awe at how big and beautiful the vacation home was. The photos and videos online did it no justice. We got out of the car and as soon as we approached the house, the owner walked out. My glee suddenly went dim upon seeing the flustered look on her face. We got out of the car, approaching her, hoping for good news.

"Ms. Artello. Hi, I'm Janet," she greeted me.

"Hi. Well, you already know me, and this is my best friend, Porsha, and my sister, Remi."

"Nice to meet you, ladies. Uh, I have something I'd like to discuss."

"Is everything okay?" I quizzed.

"No, it's not. I'm so sorry for what I'm about to tell you."

"What is it?"

"I was out of town on business, and my daughter was

handling my Airbnb business while I was gone. It has come to my attention that she has double booked the house."

"What? Are you serious?" I asked, with wide eyes. I may have been a little dramatic when I said I would stay in a roach hotel for a week, but I didn't truly mean it.

"I'm so sorry. This is also my last Airbnb. Three other people paid to stay here as well for a week."

"So, what does that mean for us?"

"I can give you half of your money back, and you guys can share the Airbnb for the week. And next time you're here, I'll give you a discount."

"Share? Does it look like we wanna share a damn house with strangers?"

"I mean, it is a six-bedroom, five bathroom. It's pretty spacious. That's all I can do for you right now, unless you'd like a complete refund."

"Get a complete refund and do what? Everywhere else is booked; there's literally not one good hotel here that we can stay in for a week."

"I'm sorry yet again. I've never had this happen before."

"Your daughter needs her ass whipped," said Porsha.

"Can you give us a minute, please?" I asked. She nodded before Remi, Porsha, and I stepped to the side.

"So, what are we gonna do?" asked Remi.

"I was going to ask the same thing," I sighed.

"What if these people are a bunch of fucking creeps?" Porsha quizzed.

"Look, we already drove two hours to get here. If they're a bunch of creeps, I have my gun and my taser, and I'm not afraid to use it. Everything is booked. Plus, it's Bike Week too."

They looked hesitant at first before agreeing to stay. After settling things with the owner, we went inside to tour the house and pick our rooms before the other people came. I sat on my bed before running my hands down my face. Remi and Porsha came in with weak smiles on their faces.

"You okay?" askd Porsha.

"Somewhat. I just didn't expect this."

"Girl, like you said, we are going to have some fucking fun regardless, period," said Remi.

"I hope so."

"Hold up, I just thought of something."

"Wassup, P?"

"If all six rooms are being taken up, where Darnell dirty dick ass sleeping at?"

"With his girlfriend," I simply replied, squinting my eyes at Remi.

"He's sleeping on the couch. I told y'all we just talking for right now."

"Y'all fucking. Quit lying to your damn sister."

"Look, I got a bottle of Crown in my suitcase; let's start this trip off right."

They smiled at me before following me to the living room. Pulling the bottle from my suitcase, I poured us up a shot while Remi got the music started.

Cree "Trigg" Wright

"Yo baby, let me get that number!" Bozz yelled, hanging out the window of my white Land Rover.

After three long ass hours, we'd finally made it to Myrtle Beach, and I was amazed by the scenery. The exotic strips, palm trees swaying in the breeze, and the people out, just having fun with each other. I couldn't wait to get a taste of this shit. Ever since I left Charlotte, all I could do was think about my mom, but Bozz and KC took my mind off of it quickly. The whole ride here, we bumped Bagg and Kevin Gates, just talking shit to one another. My sad and gloomy mood shifted as soon as I saw the sign that said, Welcome to Myrtle Beach. I rested my arm on the window, letting that nice ocean breeze brush against my skin. We weren't even close to the ocean, and we felt that shit. I'd been up all night, just researching shit to do here. We were here for a week, and I was about to enjoy that shit before it was time for me to go back home to the hectic shit.

Nigga, hustlers don't stop, they keep goin' (yeah)

You can lose your life but it's gon' keep goin'

Why not risk life when it's gon' keep goin'? (yeah)

When you die somebody else was born

But at least we got to say

BUZZ, BUZZ, BUZZ, CLICK. I shook my head at KC ignoring yet another call on my phone as if this shit was hers. For the entire ride here, she'd been ignoring my incoming calls so she could play music. My phone rang yet again, interrupting Young Thug's "Digits".

"Man, who keep calling?" I asked.

"I don't know, but they about to get cussed the fuck out."

"Answer it next time; it might be important."

"Yeah, I doubt it. Ohhh, got damn! I know that's jelly 'cause jam don't shake like that! Hey, baby!" KC screamed out the window to a group of females who looked as if they were walking to the beach. I could already tell that Bozz and KC were going to enjoy themselves more than me. When we pulled up to the Airbnb my mom set up for us, I raised my eyebrow in suspicion at the two cars in the driveway. Bozz and KC looked just as confused.

"Maybe the owner got somebody helping her set shit up for us. This a big ass house; I know I'm gone enjoy myself. Bitches upstairs and bitches downstairs," KC smiled, rubbing her hands together. We got out of the car and grabbed our suitcases, preparing to walk in. As soon as we stepped up to the door, it swung open, revealing the owner, Janet.

"Ms. Wright, hi," she chuckled, nervously.

"Hey, how you doing?"

"I'm great. I've been calling you."

"Oh, you have?" I replied, sarcastically before looking over at KC, who held an apologetic look on her face.

"My bad, I ain't knew it was you. The number wasn't saved."

"It's fine, but we do have a bit of a problem."

"A problem?" I asked.

"That problem better be something as simple as one of the bathrooms not working," said Bozz.

"It seems as if my daughter was a bit confused on certain things when I left her in charge. The problem is, she accidentally doubled booked the house."

"Double booked?"

"Yes. I already shared this news with the other wo—"

"Other? Wait, so you telling me other people are already in there? What happened to first come first served?"

"I gave them a choice, and I'll be giving you all the same choice I gave them. I can give you back partial payment and you share the home for the week. It's very spacious, so there's plenty of room for everyone. Or, I can give you back a full refund and a discount on the next time you're here. But, just to inform you, everything is booked due to it being the beginning of Spring Break and Bike Week. Once again, I'm so sor—"

"Sorry, yeah we know," I sighed, pinching the bridge of my nose. The last thing I wanted to do was spend the week in an Airbnb with a couple of strange ass people. I'd lay a motherfucker out in a heartbeat if I felt some type of way, and I was praying whoever was inside got the gist of that. Bozz and KC looked at me, trying to figure out what move I was going to make. Shaking my head, I turned around, about to get back into my car. I knew how I could get when a motherfucker bothered me, and I had a feeling that whoever was inside was going to test my gangster. I could've been back at home, making sure my mom was straight.

"Really, man? Come on, bruh, a three hour drive, and we going back home?"

"Yo Janet, you got the information to send that refund?" I shrugged, hopping back into the driver's seat.

"Mr. Wright, maybe if you get to kno—"

"I didn't come here to get to know some roomies. Do we look like members of Jersey fucking Shore to you?" I could tell by the startled look on her face that I scared her a little, but I didn't give a damn. I was never a nigga who settled for less.

"Sir, I—"

"I get it, your daughter fucked up. Bozz, KC, let's bounce."

"Jacky, give me a second to speak to my boy real fast," said KC, walking up to me.

"It's Janet," she corrected.

"Look, I know this isn't what you expected, but brighten the fuck up, nigga. We in fucking Myrtle Beach. The sun's shining and bitches are smiling. You know what they say about friendly bitches, and I been seeing bitches smile since we passed the welcome sign. Come on, man, you just finding any excuse to go back home. Everything's going good in the streets back home, and your mom is good. Stop being a lil' bitch."

"I agree with her, man. Come on, we already here," Bozz butted in.

"When you niggas start agreeing on shit?"

"When your ass started acting like a lil' ass baby. Come on, man, give it a chance."

Shaking my head and letting out a deep sigh, I got out of the car and agreed to stay. As soon as we stepped in, you could hear the music thumping like it was a fucking kickback.

Yeah, I want your body, I need your body

Long as you got me, you won't need nobody

You want it, I got it, go get it, I buy it

Tell them other broke joker "Be quiet!"

T.I.'s "Whatever You Like" played loudly as we walked up on three women rapping loudly with shots in their hands already. One of them was standing on the island twerking, the other was rapping hard as hell like a nigga, and the last one was dancing slow, yet subtle, while sipping on whatever brown liquor was in her cup.

"Got damn!" KC yelled, catching their attention. I'd lost track of how many times her ass had yelled got damn since we touched down. They quickly turned the music down before Janet stood in the middle of the floor to get our attention.

"Well, it seems as if everyone is here. Once again, I'd like to apologize about this, and I would like to thank everyone for agreeing to these circumstances. You all are aware of the rules I set. I will be refunding half of the money back into both of your accounts this afternoon. There's a map on the fridge, along with places you guys might like to check out. Mr. Wright, this is Ms. Artello, her friend, and her sister. Ms. Artello, I would introduce you to Mr. Wright's guests, but I'm unaware of their names, my apologies."

"Oh, it's cool. I can introduce myself. Hey, lil' baby, my name is KC. I hope I can get to know you better this week," KC smiled, approaching Ms. Artello and kissing her hand.

"Uh uh, Rylee, you better watch it before that girl try and eat your coochie," said her friend.

"I'd rather eat yours," KC flirted with her.

"Okay, that's my cue," Janet laughed lightly. I watched as Janet walked out the door before bringing my attention to the ladies.

"Look, I'm not about to go around calling you Ms. Artello, so what's your name?" I asked bluntly.

"Well damn, nigga, you rude," said her friend.

"Well, let's start by you asking for my name better than that." Ms. Artello retorted.

"You don't have to tell me your real name at all. It's not like

I'm gonna be talking to you much." I simply shrugged, already not feeling her uppity attitude.

"I can sense immaturity from a mile away, so I'm gonna let that slide. My name is Rylee. That's my sister, Remi, and that's my best friend, Porsha."

"Was that so hard? I didn't think it was."

"Formality usually goes both ways."

"Well, that's my boy, Bozz, and that's KC. My name is—"

"Oh, I know exactly who you are," said Remi, walking over to me. Shawty had been eye raping me since I stepped foot in the door.

"Remi, get out of that man face," Rylee snapped.

"Your name is Trigg," she smiled, showing off her braces. She licked her lips before eyeing me up and down.

"You aware?"

"Oh, am I aware? Baby, I love your work. Did you do this?" she asked, grabbing my arm and admiring my ink.

"I did my forearm."

"Maybe you can tat me sometime this week."

"I'll think on it."

"You know why they call me KC?" KC asked Porsha, who was already fed up with her.

"I don't care," she rolled her eyes.

"It stands for Kissing Coochie. When you gone let me taste it out?"

"Stop lying to that damn girl. Her name is Katherine."

"Bozz, shut the fuck up, man!" KC yelled at him.

"Rylee, is it?" I asked.

"Yes?"

"You better watch your homegirl. KC got a way of turning bitches."

"You better watch your little stud friend. Porsha don't do much yelling before she start fucking shit up."

"Noted."

"Well, we already chose our rooms, which are all upstairs, so hopefully, that makes things easier. You guys have down, and we have up."

"I'm cool with that."

"So, Trigg, what you and your people got planned for the night?" asked Remi.

Staring her in her face for a few moments, I took in her beauty. If it wasn't for me taking it in carefully, I wouldn't have recognized her.

"I remember you," I said with a raised brow.

"Oh lord, please don't tell me this tramp fucked you too," said Porsha.

"I was trying to figure out if you were going to recognize me. You haven't replied to any of my DMs."

"I'm a busy man."

"Well, you're here with me all week, so we have all the time to talk and get to know each other," she flirted, pushing her titties up in my face.

"You know who else love talking? Your man, who's supposed to be here tomorrow, right? Remember Darnell? The nigga you said you were talking to? The nigga you invited?" said Porsha.

I laughed before walking off. I could already tell this week was going to be filled with bullshit. Porsha and Remi looked as if all they did was start shit with one another. I would've hated to have to pull my piece out and scare these hoes to make them act right, but I wasn't about to deal with bickering and bitching the whole week. I stepped outside, and Bozz soon followed.

"Brighten up, nigga. It's Spring Break," Bozz chuckled before pulling out a cigar.

"Yeah, Spring Break my ass," I sighed.

Rylee Artello

Say you my nigga, I'ma be your killer

Nobody gon' play with you when I'm with you

Go against any nigga, like fuck this glitter

Skeet off dirt, I'm ditchin'

I put it in for you, I spin for you

Whatever you with, I'm with it

How you gon' cross a nigga that rockin' with you?

I got you lit in the city

"Are you fucking serious?!" I screamed in my pillow. I looked at the nightstand. It was six in the morning. "Super Gremlin" by Kodak Black was playing so damn loud, I could hear it from upstairs.

I was slowly starting to regret staying here in the first place. One thing I didn't like was waking up early. I knew it was ironic because I was a teacher, but this was too much. I wasn't supposed to be waking up at this time of morning unless I had to deal with students. Pulling the covers from over my body, I went downstairs to see Mr. Wright and his friends, along with Porsha and Remi in the living room, rapping to the music and drinking. To say I was furious was an understatement. I was definitely about to serve this young ass nigga, whoever he was, on a platter. Just from first meeting him, I didn't like his attitude or demeanor. I'd dealt with people like him before, and his whole thug persona definitely didn't scare me.

"I'm trying to sleep!" I yelled over the music.

"Come on, big booty, join in on the fun! We got a bottles of white and brown, whatever's gone turn that sexy frown upside down!" KC yelled.

"It's six in the fucking morning! Turn it down!" I'm not the only one sleeping! We have neighbors! Janet said no loud music at a certain time!" I yelled at them.

"Come on, Rylee. Lighten up, sis," Remi slurred.

"Take your ass back to bed. We not fucking with you, so don't come down here fucking with us. You came here for the same reason we did. You wanna sleep, go to your car," said Mr. Wright.

"Boy! I will come down there and whip your as—"

"Rylee, chill. Okay, we're gonna turn it down. See, look, my bad, we sorry," said Porsha, grabbing the remote and turning the music down.

"If you ever talk to me like that again, me and you are gonna have a problem," I pointed my finger at Mr. Wright. I wasn't calling his ass Trigg. If I didn't know his first name, I was going to call him by his last name.

"Yeah, goodnight, Princess," he smooched at me. I clenched my fist before turning around and heading back to my room, slamming the door. Jumping back in bed, I tried my hardest to go back to sleep, but I couldn't. They'd already woken me up from a deep slumber, and all I could do was think about Darnell's grimy ass arriving within a few hours. Pulling my phone out, I decided to do something stupid. I knew that many people weren't up at this time, but I was hoping he was.

Me: Hey, are you up?

Drayton ❤: I am, actually.

Me: Why are you up so early?

Drayon ❤: I should be asking you the same thing, beautiful

Me: Couldn't sleep.

Drayton ❤: You know I been thinking about you.

Me: You have?

Drayton ❤: I have. Thinking about where I'm going to take you for our first date. You know I wanna be the first one to give you a tour of Georgia.

Me: Can't wait for that tour. I actually can't wait to start work.

Drayon ❤: Looks like you really love your job. It's Spring Break and you're already talking about work

Me: I can be up all night telling you how much I love my job.

Drayton ❤: And I'll be up all night listening

I thought I would have fallen asleep talking to Drayton, but I ended up staying up all morning, smiling and giggling at my phone like a lovesick schoolgirl. Putting my phone on the charger, I went downstairs to see everybody sprawled out on the couch and on the floor. After getting shit faced early in the morning, I would be sleep too. Going into the kitchen, I noticed that Janet had already had groceries in the fridge. I knew she was trying to make up for the fact that her daughter had fucked everything up. Pulling out bacon, sausage, pancake mix, and eggs, I started to cook.

"Alexa, play music," I commanded.

I wake up every morning and tell myself

Good morning, gorgeous

Sometimes you gotta look in the mirror and say

Good Morning, gorgeous

No one else could make me feel this way (yeah)

Good morning, gorgeous

"Good Morning Gorgeous" by Mary J Blige played lightly as I threw down in the kitchen. Unlike the disrespectful fuckers I was in this house with, I respected their sleep. I sang lightly to the music as I flipped the blueberry pancake in the skillet, inhaling the aroma.

"You got a nice voice," said Mr. Wright, catching me off guard.

"Shit! You can't be sneaking up on people like that. What the fuck?" I huffed, holding my chest.

"My bad, I ain't mean to scare you."

"Mhm."

"It smell good in here."

"Thanks."

"I'm assuming you only cooked for you and your girls."

"Nope, I cooked for myself. Everyone's hands work."

"Damn, punishment from last night, huh?"

"Call it what you want."

"For somebody who's a teacher, you sure got a mouthpiece on you."

"How do you kno—"

"Your sister told me."

"I bet she did."

"How old you is?"

"The correct term would be, how old are you?"

"If I wanted a fucking tutor, I would have paid for one," he shrugged.

"I'm thirty-two," I rolled my eyes at his ignorance.

"You sound like you from Charleston," he chuckled, lightly leaning on the counter.

"How?"

"You sounded Geechee as hell when you were yelling at us," he laughed to himself.

Standing back, I finally got a good look at him. We shared the same skin tone, and he looked as if he stayed in the gym on his bad days. His waves were deeper than the ocean that was behind the house, and his beard looked like he moisturized it daily in the purest shea butter. He had one sleeve, and the tattoos that cascaded down that one arm looked as if Picasso had done it himself. He was damn sure a prize to look at, but his attitude and demeanor were what dimmed his light.

"So, you do tattoos?"

"I do," he nodded his head.

"How long you been tattooing?"

"Since I was sixteen. My uncle taught me. I actually did my first piece on him. I work at his shop back home. A lot of people come to get tatted by me. Devious Ink is the best spot to get your ink at in Charlotte."

"Look at you promoting," I laughed lightly.

"Look at you burning shit up."

"Shit!" I yelled, turning around and turning the stove off. My eggs were now overcooked and sticking to the pan.

"Your mouth always been this smart?"

"You always been this uptight?"

"You call it uptight; I call it mature."

"Well, Ms. Mature, me and my folks going to Carolina's Pancake House. Enjoy your breakfast, love," he said before walking off, leaving me looking stupid. Shaking my head, I threw my eggs in the trash before going to the table to eat the rest of my food. Just like he said, he and his friends went out to get breakfast. I would have that thought Remi and Porsha would have kept me company, but they went with them, leaving me in this big ass house alone. I went into my bedroom and changed out of my clothes and into a cheetah print two piece. After pinning my hair into a tight bun, I grabbed a towel and went out to the patio to get into the pool. As I dipped my toe in, I felt a shudder glide down my spine from the cold temperature. I got in slowly, letting my body get accustomed to the water. I began to float on my back, listening to the seagulls squawk over my head as they flew above me. Closing my eyes, I took in the peace I had been longing for.

"I see you still love to float on your back."

I damn near drowned turning around to see who was talking. Standing back on my feet, I was face to face with Darnell, who was sitting in one of the chairs by the pool. The peace I once thought I had vanished just that fast. Getting out of the pool, I rolled my eyes and wrapped my towel around my body so he could stop gawking at me.

"Damn, no hello?"

"I didn't invite you," I shrugged.

"It's been a minute."

"That's a good thing."

"I heard you're moving."

"Why are you talking to me? Matter fact, why even are you breathing?"

"I deserve that."

"You deserve a lot of bad things, but I'm trying my hardest to not be the bitter ex 'cause I'm far from that."

"Rylee, can we talk?"

"We have nothing to talk about."

"We have a lot to talk about."

"No, we don't. Now if you'll excuse me, I was just heading in."

"Don't let me ruin your swim."

"You ruined my whole trip by just being here."

"I'm here because I still love you."

"Aren't you fucking my sister? I see you love fucking sisters," I laughed to myself.

"Don't do that."

"Do what? Tell the truth? Darnell, if you wanna make me happy, and I mean truly make me happy, leave," I simply replied, walking off, but he grabbed my arm, towering over me. His grip was so tight, I could feel my circulation cutting off that fast.

"Get your hands off me." I tried to yank away, but he grabbed me harder and pulled me close.

"That's why we didn't work out in the beginning. You don't know how to fucking listen. I said I fucking love you, Rylee, don't you know that?" he said through gritted teeth, staring me in my eyes.

"Let me go," I whimpered.

Hearing the doors open, he let me go. I damn near busted

my ass running into the house, trying to get away from Darnell's psychotic ass. Mr. Wright grabbed me, and I almost knocked his head off his shoulders, but he stepped back.

"You good?" he asked, seeing the worry on my face.

"I'm fine, I'm just fine," I simply replied, rushing back to my room. I took a quick shower before throwing on something comfortable. As soon as I walked back into my bedroom, Porsha and Remi were sitting on my bed.

"You okay?" asked Porsha.

"Why wouldn't I be?" I asked.

"I saw Darnell's bitch ass downstairs."

"I'm fine, I'm not stunting him."

"I feel bad. I feel like I shouldn't have even invited him," Remi pouted.

"It's fine, I'm fine. I'm not worried about him."

"Good, now let's change the subject. Let's talk about Trigg's fine, sexy ass. Woah God, the thing's I'd do to that man. I'll get him pregnant," Remi fanned herself.

"Didn't you invite Darnell? How are you just comfortably talking about another man?" I quizzed.

"Me and Darnell are not together; we just talk. How many times do I have to tell you this?" she smiled.

"If you say so," I sighed.

"Enough about Darnell, back to Trigg's fine ass. Oh my God," Remi fanned herself.

"I wonder if you walk in church do it get hot?" Porsha questioned.

"What are you talking about?"

"You ever heard the term 'it's hotter than a whore in church?' I just wanted to know if it's true."

"I would cuss you out for that, but I don't care. I'll be Trigg's hoe."

"Remi, that's nasty. You don't even know that man, and you tryna sleep with him?"

"And is," she flipped her hair.

"I guess," I shrugged.

"Have you not seen that man's body? Ohh girl, and he a gangster," she fanned herself.

"Oh hell nah, and you think that makes it better?" I looked at her in disgust.

"Girl fuck you, chill with that. He's not like that, though."

"How do you know what he's like if you don't know him?"

"Listen, just know he's about his business, and he packin'. He's the leader of the Red Havens."

"Never heard of them. Can we talk about something else other than dick?"

"I got something. Remi, tell her what we talked about at breakfast." I looked over at Porsha, who rolled her eyes at Remi. I knew from the looks on their faces, the news wasn't good.

"Really, Porsha?"

"Don't really me; she deserves to know."

"To know what?"

"Your sister wanna play follow the leader. She's going to the college you're going to be teaching at."

I looked at Remi, ready to punch her in her face.

Cree "Trigg" Wright

"I'm about to see what shawty up to," said KC, licking her lips and flipping her collar on her button-down Tommy Hilfiger polo shirt. She and Bozz had gotten dressed up and were ready to hit the strip while I was still in some sweats and Nike hoodie. I was in a bad mood after getting a call from KC's mom about my mom not doing too well. My mom had fainted and hit her head on the kitchen counter, and I wanted to leave and take care of her. I was grateful for KC's mom being next door. After the incident, she decided to stay with my mom until the trip was over. My anxiety was to the fucking roof, and even if I wanted to have fun, I couldn't.

"Leave Porsha alone before she fuck you up. She already said she don't swing that way."

"You know I'm known for turning bitches out. I bet you a band I'll have her ass wrapped around me like a magnum before the trip ends."

"I gotta see that. I'm down; I'll add another band to it," said Bozz, fixing his Ray-Bans.

"Shit, why not? I bet you too," I chuckled lightly. KC was right. She would turn the straightest bitch out, but Porsha was something serious. She was feisty, and little did she know, that shit drove KC crazy.

"You niggas about to get me paid. I already got shawty coming with me to Broadway at the Beach."

"Ah shit, I see you, playa," Bozz dapped her up.

As soon as we heard Porsha coming down the stairs, our conversation came to a halt. I stroked my beard as I eyed shawty up and down. She was bad, but her attitude threw me off. Her outfit was casual and simple compared to the last outfit she had on when she first arrived. Porsha sported a gray Bugs Bunny crop top, light blue ripped jeans where you could see her ass perfectly, and a pair of gray Chucks.

"Shhh. Be vewy vewy quiet. I'm hunting wabbits, " KC imitated Elmer Fudd.

"Shut up. Come on, Elmer Studd, before I change my mind," Porsha rolled her eyes.

KC opened the door for her before watching her walk out. She stuck her tongue out at both of us before running after Porsha. I then looked over at Bozz, who was about to walk out with them.

"Damn brody, they got you third wheeling?" I laughed.

"Who said shit about a third wheel? I'm tryna get at Remi fine ass. Porsha got her to tag along with us."

"After all that yelling and shit between her and her sister, I'd wanna get the fuck outta here too. Sound like she was ripping her sister a new ass hole."

"Yeah, that argument was heated."

"Mind y'all business," said Remi, coming down the steps.

"The princess has finally arrived. Come on, baby girl. We about to head out."

"Mhm, I'm coming. Trigg, you coming with?" she asked.

"Nah, I'm gone stay here."

"What? Why? That's the only reason I was coming. I thought you were coming. He said—"

"Don't listen to shit Bozz says. Maybe next time. Go have fun, baby girl. I'm good right here for now."

She looked hurt before storming out to the car. Bozz shrugged before following her out. Remi was getting on my nerves, little did she know. Shawty was cool, but one thing I hated was a clingy bitch, and that's what she was. She was trying too hard to be seen, and sadly, I was tired of seeing her. I wondered heavily why she was all on my dick when she invited a nigga she was supposedly fucking with here. That said a lot, and the last thing I wanted to do was bust somebody's head to the white meat over a bitch — especially a bitch I didn't want. That nigga left the house early this morning, and I was glad. I didn't like how he looked at me, and I was a man of action — not words.

"Mama! I swear to God I'm gonna kill her! She does this every time. I should have never agreed to let her come here! Ever since she's been here, she's been ruining everything!" Rylee yelled.

She sounded mad as hell, and I could tell Remi had pushed her to her limit with how bad shit sounded earlier today between them. Once the yelling ceased, I stood up and walked upstairs to check on her. I was the only motherfucker in this house that was supposed to be having a fucked up time, and I didn't like competition. Going towards the door, I knocked, and it swung open, revealing her short ass.

"If you came up here to get on my ass about yelling, right now isn't the time."

"I was tryna be a nice motherfucker for once and check on you, but take your mean ass back in there and stay in your feelings," I shrugged, about to walk off, but she grabbed me.

"Look, I'm sorry, it's just that Remi really pissed—"

"Pissed you off? I heard. You wanna talk about it?"

"I really don't. This was supposed to be a trip where I finally got some peace after a being around kids damn near every day, and now I have Remi fucking shit up."

"Get dressed," I sighed.

"What?"

"You heard, get dressed and pack a bathing suit. I'm not gone tell you again."

I walked off towards my room before changing into a white tee, my blue Ralph Lauren shorts, and my all white Yeezys. After washing my face and making sure my waves were on point, I moisturized my beard with pure shea butter that my mother had taught me how to make from scratch. Clapping my hands together and standing back in the mirror, I smiled, impressed with my 'fit. Grabbing my phone off the charger, I then went downstairs to see Rylee already dressed and ready.

"Damn," I mumbled, tracing my tongue across my bottom lip. She sported an Orlando jersey dress that had slits on the side with a pair of all white Forces. I was about to make myself known until that Darnell nigga walked through the door with bags in his hands. When he saw Rylee, he had the same look on his face that I had.

"Where you goin'?" he asked, placing the bags on the couch.

"None of your business, Darnell."

"It is my business."

"Don't start with me today. Shouldn't you be up my sister's ass?"

"Rylee, you gone keep throwing that in my face?"

"Hmm, I don't know; you tell me. Should I be happy that you not only cheated on me with your stepsister, but you're now fucking on my baby sister? Then, you had the nerve to ease your way into a trip you weren't invited to. Darnell, find the nearest cliff and jump. And make sure to do a flip." She tried to walk away from him, but he grabbed her, pulling her back to him.

"Didn't I tell you to watch how the fuck you talk to me?"

Putting my hand on my piece, I walked down, and he let her go.

"Nah nigga, don't let her go now. Keep doing that bold shit you were doing before I walked down," I said, standing in front of Rylee.

"This ain't got shit to do with yo' young ass. Go sit your ass down somewhere, lil' nigga."

"You must don't know who the fuck you dealing with."

"Stop, come on. Ignore him, let's go. You said we were going somewhere, right? Let's go, please," Rylee pleaded, holding onto my arm for dear life. Seeing the fear in her eyes, I let out a deep chuckle before stepping back and grabbing my keys.

"You fucking this lil' ass boy? That's what we doing now, Rylee?" Darnell said in disgust.

"Ignore his punk ass. Come on."

I grabbed her arm and walked her towards my car. Once we got in, I wasted no time in putting my destination into the GPS and driving off. We sat in silence because neither of us knew what to say to each other. As bad as I hated getting out of character, it had to happen. One thing I hated was bitch ass niggas who abused women, and when I heard that shit, it ate me up inside. All I could think about were my little sisters when I saw that shit.

"Thank you," she said in a low tone.

"You don't have to thank me. As long as we in the same house, you ain't gotta worry about that shit happening again," I shrugged.

"No, thank you, really. I didn't expect you to step in. You

didn't have to."

"And if I didn't step in, what was going to happen next? He rock your shit and kill you?"

"Why did you jump in, if you don't mind me asking? It's clear we're not fans of each other, so why take up for me?"

"My sister."

"What?"

"My sister was dating this older dude, and she kept that shit away from me and my parents. You a smart girl. You a teacher; you can put two and two together. I been running Red Haven for quite some time. Her nigga came to me wanting to be in on gang, and I wouldn't let him in. He called himself trying to get back at me by fucking with my sister. He used to beat her ass. I threatened his bitch ass and made my sister stop fucking with him. One day, he caught me lackin'. He tried to shoot me, but my sister jumped in the way and saved me. I blame myself for that shit every day. I could have saved her when he was beating her ass. I could have saved her that night; she wasn't even supposed to be there."

I gripped the steering wheel as I was brought back to that night. I sooner calmed my nerves, coming to the realization that I'd just talked about the situation. I hadn't talked about what happened to Kimmy since that night, and here I was, telling this girl I barely knew about what went down effortlessly.

"It's not your fault," she said, placing her hand on my shoulder.

"It was, and I know it was. But I'm still trying to live and get over that shit."

"You can't get over something like that so easy. I know it's hard."

"You have no idea how hard that shit is," I sighed.

"Mr. Wright, I—"

"Don't call me that. Shit sounds like I'm still in high school," I laughed at her professionalism.

"Well, I'm not calling you Trigg. Sound like a street thug."

"I'm not a thug," I laughed.

"Then what are you?"

"Baby girl, I'm a gangsta," I stroked my beard.

"Well, Mr. Gangsta, I will be calling you Mr. Wright until you tell me your real name."

"Damn, you difficult. You can tell you a teacher," I laughed.

"You know my name, so I think it's fair if you tell me yours."

"Fine, if it'll help that pretty little head sleep better at night. My name's Creshawn, but people call me Cree. Let me rephrase that. People who I really care about call me Cree."

"See, that wasn't so hard," she smiled, nudging my shoulder.

"You goofy."

"How old are you, though?"

"Twenty-three."

"Oh no. Boy, let me out this car."

"Watch it with that boy shit. You only nine years older than me; chill that shit out. I'm a grown ass man, and I wear that shit proudly."

"I didn't know you were that young."

"How old did you think I was?"

"At least in your late twenties. You're still a baby," she laughed lightly.

"Watch it. I'm tryna be respectful."

"Mhm, so what brings you to Myrtle Beach, if you don't mind me asking."

"Spring Break, obviously. I ain't even wanna come, if you want me to be real."

"If you didn't wanna come, why come? Did your friends make you?"

"My mom did," I sighed.

"Wait, let me get this straight. Your mom made you come to Myrtle Beach for Spring Break? This is my first time hearing somebody's mother tell them to go out and have fun."

"She has cancer."

"Oh, I'm sor—"

"I'm sorry too. I spend most of my time taking care of her, and she thought I needed a break."

"Smart woman."

"Yeah, she is," I smiled.

"Aight, you invited me out to have fun, and it looks like you need to have some fun yourself. So, let's do that. Let's see what's on this radio," she replied, turning the radio up to the max. Biggie's "One More Chance" blasted through the speakers loudly, and her face lit up.

First things first: I, Poppa, freaks all the honeys

Dummies, Playboy bunnies, those wanting money

Those the ones I like 'cause they don't get nathan

But penetration

Unless it smells like sanitation

Gar-bage, I turn like doorknobs

Heart throb never, Black and ugly as ever

"Ahh shit, this is my song! However, I stay Coogi down to the socks! Rings and watch filled with rocks!" she rapped.

"And my jam knock in your Mitsubishi. Girls pee-pee when they see me. Navajos creep me in they teepee," I joined in.

"Uh uh, boy what you know about Biggie?!" she exclaimed, making me laugh.

"Oh, you one of those. Calm your ass down. Wasn't you like three when this came out?"

"Wasn't you in yo' daddy's nuts when this came out? At least I was here," she flicked me off.

"You and this smart ass mouth."

"Ok so?" she laughed.

We sang to damn near every song that came on while talking shit to each other before we arrived at Myrtle Beach Safari. It was packed as a bitch out here. Getting out, Rylee and I walked inside before exploring damn near the entire safari.

"Miss, would you like to take a picture with our little buddy, Bananas?" the park's tour guide asked Rylee. She smiled before nodding and handing me her phone. The monkey jumped on her shoulders before playing with her hair. I couldn't help but to smile at how happy she was.

"If it piss on you, don't look crazy. The house is all the way on the other side of town."

"Do these monkeys pee on people?" she asked the guide with wide eyes. Just from the look on her face, that answered the question. Rylee damn near threw the monkey back at the lady. Rylee and I had fed one of the park's African Elephants named

Bubbles, and we even got our pictures and videos taken of us playing with the lion cubs.

"I heard you can swim with tigers and paint with monkeys too," said Rylee, showing me a video on her phone of a couple swimming with the tigers.

"Look, no disrespect, but I'm not swimming with no damn tiger. What if it eat our ass, on some National Geographic shit?" I understood she wanted the whole experience, but I wasn't the nigga to experiment new shit with.

"Come on, Cree, please?" she pouted.

"Rylee, I don't know," I looked hesitantly.

"Stop being a baby."

"You right about that one."

"Look, you can hold my hand the entire time."

"Rylee," I warned.

"Please," she begged.

Sighing, I finally gave him. We went to one of the guides, who was putting the monkey away.

"Hey, how much does it cost to swim with the tigers and shit?" I asked.

"Excuse me?"

"I'm sorry, he meant how much does it cost to swim with tigers and paint with the chimps?" Rylee asked.

"I said that," I raised my eyebrow at her.

"Um, sadly, you can't do a walk in; you have to book ahead. And it costs $689 per person."

"Oh, okay, maybe next time."

"We have an opening for tomorrow at 9 a.m.," she said.

"We'll take it," said Rylee.

After making an appointment for tomorrow, Rylee and I went to Ella's Ice Cream before walking the strip. I didn't know who the fuck Ella was, but I needed her to give me this ice cream recipe to take back to Charlotte.. Rylee and I had been out so long, we'd lost track of time. We'd been around each other since ten this morning and got back into the house around eleven. We even had dinner at this bomb ass seafood restaurant called Crabby Mikes. All the hell I gave my mom about not wanting to go really made me feel stupid. I was having a hell of a good time, and if it wasn't for Rylee, I would've been back at the house, downing whatever brown I could get my hands on. She was growing on me, but I knew I had to shake that shit out of my head. We would only be around each other for this week, and after that, we were back to our separate lives.

"You ever been with a big nigga before?" Bozz asked, leaning on my door frame.

It was one in the morning, and I was feeling salty as hell. After hearing that Rylee's uptight ass spent the entire day with Trigg, I was fuming. Porsha's special ed ass was getting her coochie licked by the stud, and Bozz's fat, ugly ass had been trying to get with me since he first laid eyes on me. I was hoping and praying that he would walk his big overgrown ass next door to Rylee's room, and they hooked up instead. I was on a mission, and that mission was to get Trigg. When I found out that he was coming to Myrtle Beach for Spring Break, I wasted no time in begging Rylee to have me tag along. The only problem was, I didn't expect for this mix up to happen and end up staying in the same house.

"Bozz, no disrespect, but get the hell away from my door," I rolled my eyes.

"Damn, I fed you good, bought you what you wanted, and treated you good, and you still giving a nigga the cold shoulder?"

"I don't like you, okay?"

"Why? Is it 'cause I'm fat?"

"Nah, it's because you're ugly and fat. Now get the fuck away from my door," I spat.

"You a bitch, you know that, right?"

"I've been told."

"I hope somebody beat your ass."

"Boy, bye," I fanned him off.

As soon as he walked away, Darnell walked in, making me roll my eyes. I got rid of one headache, and then the migraine decided to walk in. He closed my door, making sure to lock it behind him.

"What do you want, Darnell?" I asked in annoyance.

"We need to talk."

"About?"

"Your sister."

"What did she do now?"

"She fuckin' that nigga?"

"She better not be," I replied, getting amped.

"I ain't like how he rolled up on me. You better get your lil' boy toy before I break his fucking jaw. The only reason I'm here is to get Rylee back, and that's what I'm gonna do."

"How's that going?" I scoffed, knowing it wasn't going well.

The only reason he was here was to patch things back up with Rylee. A while back, after he and Rylee's relationship ended, we started messing around. Darnell had good dick; I'd give him that, but that was all I wanted from him. We lost contact until recently. When he found out I was going with Rylee to Myrtle Beach, he came up with an elaborate scheme to get her back. We combined our plans together, and in the end, I would end up with Trigg, and he would have that bullshit ass fairytale ending he wanted with my sister.

"You know it's not going well."

"I mean, what do you expect, Darnell? Do you not know yourself?"

"The fuck do you mean by that?"

"You put your hands on my sister, cheat on her, then get mad when she won't take you back."

"That was then."

"Yeah, whatever."

"You got the nerve to sit in front of me and fucking judge me?"

"Call it what you want."

"Bitch, you can't judge me when you're just as fucking triflin'."

"What are you talking about?"

"You wanna sit in front of me and fucking judge me, but you're the biggest hoe I've ever met. You sucked and fucked me, what, three weeks after me and your sister and I ended things? Then, your grimy ass agreed to invite me here to get your sister back so you can fuck on a nigga that don't want you."

"Fuck you," I spat.

"Nah, fuck you. Don't get in your feelings when shit hits the fan."

"Get out," I pointed at the door.

"We're not done talking." Standing up, I approached him and gave him a look that would put him six feet under.

"You may be used to bossing Rylee's dumb ass around, but I'm different. Don't get mad at me because she doesn't want your narcissistic ass. And you calling me a hoe, but at least I'm not fucking delusional That's probably why my sister don't want your stupid ass."

Catching me off guard, he wrapped his hands around my neck and pinned me down on my bed. I clawed at his hands, gasping for air as I stared into his rage-filled eyes. When he saw I was on the brink of passing out, he let me go. I gasped for air, rubbed at my throat, and let out a fit of coughs. I was astonished that this nigga had really put his hands on me.

"Next time I'll break your fucking neck. I'll have your sister back whether she like it or not. Recognize who you fucking with. That mouth is gonna get you killed. Seems like the only thing it's good for is talking shit and sucking dick. Stick to one of those," he spat before walking out of my room, leaving me there looking dumbfounded.

I wanted so badly to run to Rylee and tell her everything, but I knew she was going to get on my ass. Matter fact, I knew she would hate me if I told her my motive behind this trip. She already felt some type of way about me going back to college. I didn't expect the news of me attending college in Georgia to make her upset like that. She barely said a word to me. If she was barely talking to me now, I knew I would be on thin ice if I told her this. I was about to get up and close my door before Porsha came in, taking off her earrings.

"Look, I don't have time for this shit right now, Porsha. If you came in here to talk shit, I—"

My sentence was cut short by Porsha punching me in my face so hard, I flew back.

Rylee Artello

"Rylee! Get this bitch off me!" Remi screamed.

I damn near broke my neck trying to get off my bed. When I went next door to Remi's room, Porsha was on top of her, beating her ass like she stole something. I ran up and tried my best to grab Porsha off of her, but she elbowed me in my chest, making me fall back. Thankfully, KC was behind me to catch me because I would've been on the damn floor. I asked these bitches not to go at each other's throats, and here they were, fucking each other up.

"Oh shit!" yelled KC, running up. Her tall ass scooped Porsha up like it was nothing before dragging her out the room, kicking and screaming. I looked at Remi, whose lace front was damn near ripped in half, and her lip was busted.

"You need to control your crazy ass friend!" she screamed. Staring into my eyes, she began to burst into tears. My big sister's instincts kicked in, and I walked over and pulled her into a hug. I felt like I was comforting her after she got her ass beat by my parents after doing something stupid. Whatever she did to piss Porsha off had to be major. I knew Porsha had beef with Remi, but one thing she wasn't going to do was fight her just because she didn't like her; there had to be something else.

"I should whip her ass!" Remi screamed.

Once I calmed her down and she cried herself to sleep like a little ass kid, I stormed off to Porsha's room. When I opened the door, she was in bed with KC with her feet kicked up in her lap.

"I'm gone give y'all some time to talk," said KC, removing Porsha's feet from her lap. KC gave me a head nod and patted my shoulder before walking out and leaving Porsha and me alone.

"The big sister in me wanna beat your ass like you stole something just for putting your hands on her like that. But the best friend in me wants to hear you out because I know your crazy ass don't show out without reason. What was that about?"

"She better be glad you walked in because I was gone beat her ass black and blue."

"Porsha!" I warned.

"Look, your sister is fucking grimy, and she deserved what I did. It's not my place to tell you the details, but just know, I walked up and heard some shit. I did it for you."

"You did it for me? Porsha, you could have come to me and talked to me about this. You know how Remi can get."

"And the bitch knows how I can get. I ain't gone touch her no more; I'm all tired out."

"I hope so. Next time, I'm fucking the both of you up. This conversation isn't over with. I had a good ass day, and I'm not letting you and Remi ruin that. So, I'm just going to change the subject," I sighed.

"I saw you was out with Trigg." She wiggled her eyebrows.

"Just how you was all booed up with KC when I walked in here."

"Don't start. I already feel weird about that."

"You let her hit?"

"You gone laugh at me?" she pouted.

"Bitch, no! Are you serious?! When?"

"We didn't do anything, yet. She kissed me, that's all. But we almost did it."

"Mhm, whatever."

"Almost doesn't count. Now back to you and Trigg. You let him put his thumb in your butt?" she asked with a stupid look on her face.

"Girl, if you don't go find some business."

"Mhm whatever. But we're all going to Family Kingdom tomorrow night, so be ready and throw on your cutest fit."

"I'm down."

"Girl, you got no choice but to be down. What are you doing tomorrow morning? I wanna check out Conway. Maybe we can get some massages and sip on some cocktails."

"I'm actually going to be busy tomorrow morning."

"Doing what?"

"Me and Cree are going back to the safari again."

"Ohhh, let me find out," she smiled.

"Shut up. We had fun today; that's why we're going again tomorrow."

"Girl, fuck that, I'm talking about you calling him Cree. That man goes by Trigg."

"His name is Cree," I smiled.

"Oh hell nahh, let me find the fuck out!" she squealed.

"Shut up, Porsha," I laughed.

"Girl, when a hood nigga tell you his real name, you already locked in. I'm here for it. Let me find out you tryna get a young nigga."

"Girl, shut up. It's just something about him."

"That dick!"

"That's it, goodnight. You running out."

After talking with Porsha for a few, I went back to my bed and tried to go to sleep, but I couldn't even do that. I was thinking about how much fun I had, I didn't even reply to any of Drayton's calls or texts.

"Creshawn, if you don't jump in this damn water."

"What if it bite me?"

"It's not," I laughed. His big, bad ass done petted the tigers and lions, and as soon as it was time to get in the water with them, he drew the line.

"Get in without me; I'll jump in after."

"Fine," I shrugged.

I jumped right in the water and began swimming with the tigers. It was definitely an experience, and I couldn't wait to visit my students and brag about this. I fluffed the big tiger's ears around and quickly moved my head when it tried to lick me in my face. I then swam over to Cree, who had his feet hanging in the water. Placing my hands on both sides of him, I looked up into his eyes.

"You're really not going to get in the water with me?"

"I don't fuck with lions like that."

"Those are tigers. There's a difference," I laughed.

"They're both big ass cats."

"Would you get mad if I dragged you in?"

"Would you get mad if I fucked you up for draggin' me in?"

"I would."

"You just answered your own question," he laughed.

"Come on, Cree. It would be a waste of money if you don't get in."

He looked hesitant before sighing and getting in the water with me. I laughed at the nervous look on his face when the tiger started swimming close to him. Once he got comfortable, we swam with the tigers for a few minutes before painting with the monkeys. After our private encounter was over, Cree and I went to the beach.

"So, Ms. Artello, I got a question for you."

"Wassup?" I laughed lightly.

"How does such a beautiful, intelligent woman end up with someone like him?"

"Stupidity is always evident, no matter the age. Love makes you do stupid things, and the dumbest thing I did was stay."

"All that matters is you're out."

"You're right about that. I just wish he would just leave me alone. Just leave in general. I don't want him here. It's like I have so much fun, and then I come back to the house to see his ass, and it ruins my mood."

"He fuck with you again, he leaving in a body bag, I know that."

"Cree, stop it. I don't want you getting in trouble."

"I love it when you say my name." He licked his juicy lips before showcasing that Colgate smile.

"Boy, you better stop," I laughed.

"I better stop what?" he asked, leaning closer. I laughed nervously before stepping back. As bad as I wanted to step into the danger zone, I couldn't do that. This man had sex appeal out the ass, and I tried my best to control myself when we were swimming together not long ago. His body was amazing, and his voice could melt butter.

"You know exactly what you're doing, and I'm not about to play with you."

"Who's playing?"

"Cree," I warned.

"Rylee." He said my name so low and seductive, I damn near nutted just from that. He pulled me into his lap, and all I could think about was if my ass was crushing him.

"Cree, I'm too big to be sitting on your lap," I said, trying to get up, but he pulled me back down.

"I'm a grown ass man; I already told you this. I carry the weight of the world on my shoulders daily. A little ass ain't gonna crush me."

He massaged my thighs, and I was about to lean in and kiss his ass, but I knew I didn't want to start anything I couldn't finish. Why start something with him when after this week was up, we'd go back to our separate lives? I assumed he saw the saddened look on my face because he grabbed me by my face and made me look at him.

"What's on your mind?" he asked.

"You."

"Me? What about me?"

"I don't want to go there with you when after the week is up, we're probably not gonna talk to each other anymore."

"Don't talk like that."

"But—"

"Listen, if it's like that, at least you can say you spent Spring Break in Myrtle Beach with a gangsta," he smirked. I straddled him before leaning into him and pressing my lips to his.

Cree "Trigg" Wright

"I bet you they fucking," KC elbowed Bozz.

They had been talking about Rylee and me ever since she and I had gotten back from the beach. All I could do was shake my head and laugh at their stupidity.

"I don't say shit about you fucking Porsha," I shrugged.

"Don't worry about me and my lil' squirter."

"I ain't need to know that," I laughed, shaking my head.

"Man, somebody gone trade bitches with me. Remi ass almost got knocked the fuck out. She a two- faced bitch."

"How is she two-faced?" asked KC.

"After your little scissor buddy whipped her ass, she came crying to me, wanting to chill with ya boy."

"From all that screaming and shit, it sounds like Porsha did a number on her."

"She did. I had to drag her ass out of there. She almost took Rylee out with her."

"Damn," I laughed.

"Don't change the subject, motherfucker. What's really up with you and ol' girl?" said Bozz.

"You niggas wanted me to have fun and enjoy myself, that's what I'm doing," I shrugged.

"That's not answering the question, nigga. We saw you caking it up with her thick ass on the beach. We saw all that ass on ya boy. Trust me, we ain't mad at cha, playa," Bozz laughed.

"It ain't nothing like that."

"Then what is it? You sure got all of us thinking something else."

"Look, she cool people, and I fuck with her. She had shit going on, and you know I got shit on my mind. We made the best out of our situations."

"I bet you did. You hit it yet?"

"If I did, I wasn't gone tell you motherfuckers," I laughed.

Our conversation was cut short by my phone going off on the table. Picking it up, I noticed my dad's name flashing on the screen. Putting my finger up at Bozz and KC to give me a minute, I then walked outside. Sliding my finger across the screen, I then placed it to my ear.

"You know how to use a phone? That's good to know," I stated, shaking my head. I had been trying to get in touch with his ass for the longest, and his ass had been dodging me like a virus. Me and my dad's relationship was cordial, but shit like this made me wanna back away completely.

"I'm a busy man, you know that."

"Too busy to check on your son and see how things are going with your ex-wife?"

"I had a lot going on. Come on, Cree, you know that."

"As bad as I wanna get on your ass about being inconsistent, I'm not going to. I care about my mom too much to be on this phone going back and forth with you about shit you already know. She's been tryna contact you abou—"

"We already talked, and that's why I'm calling you."

"Aight, good."

"Cree, we have to talk about something very important."

"Important like?"

"We both know your mom doesn't have much longer."

"Don't talk about her like that. She's still alive."

"Creshawn, you're not listening, son."

"And neither are you. If you're gonna talk about her, talk about her like she's still here," I replied, getting defensive. I knew my mom didn't have much longer, and every time it was brought up, that shit ate me up inside.

"Michelle and I talked about you on the phone for an hour."

"What about me?"

"She wants you to come to Georgia and be closer to me."

"Nah, that ain't happening."

"Cree, it's what your mother wants. I want what's best for you; she wants what's best for you. Cree, you could move here to Georgia with me, get a nice spot, and go back to school. Money is good here. You can even open up your own tattoo spot here. I know you're tired of working at Tony's."

"You got this shit already thought out, huh?"

"I care about you and your future. I know you wanna go back to school. You were close to getting your degree before you dropped out."

"That was the old me. I'm good in Charlotte."

"You're good in Charlotte? You think I don't know what you're doing? You wanna be this street thug your entire fucking life?! A fucking gangster! I know about Red Haven, Cree."

"You don't know shit about Red Haven," I spat.

"I know that that's the same fucking reason your sister is dead! I don't want that for you! You have to grow up, son! Your mother isn't going to be here much longer! I lost your sister, and I'm about to lose your mother! Don't make me go through losing you too!"

"I got me; you don't have to worry 'bout me."

"Hardheaded, just like your mother. Fine, it's gonna be like that?"

"It's exactly like that." I pinched the bridge of my nose, trying to calm down.

"This won't be our last time talking about this. I'll give you some time to think on it."

"I don't need time," I simply replied before hanging up.

I decided to stay outside to calm myself down before going back inside. I couldn't even do that before I heard Rylee yelling with someone. Going back inside, I saw Bozz holding KC back from trying to get at Darnell.

"Fuck is yo' problem, man?! Don't ever in your fucking life talk to her like that, bitch ass nigga!" KC yelled, trying to get past Bozz.

"The fuck going on?" I asked, looking between Porsha, Rylee, Bozz, and KC.

"He was talking to Rylee wild and shit, and Porsha got on his ass. I wasn't gone say shit until he walked up on Porsha like he was gone do some big dog shit! You touch that one, nigga, we scrappin' for real! I put that shit on the set!" KC was so mad, her light skin complexion was now bright red.

"This ain't got shit to do with your ass. You motherfuckers

in this house don't know how to shut the fuck up and mind your business. You niggas ain't gone stop until I set an example. I don't fucking play with kids. Just because you're dressed like a nigga don't make you one. Let her go."

I was getting sick and tired of this Darnell nigga, and I was about to show him exactly who the fuck I was. Me and my crew knew each other so well; all I had to do was give them a look, and we already knew what we were on. The three of us walked up on this nigga before going blow after blow, beating this nigga's ass like he stole something. Bozz and KC dragged his ass outside to the pool, and I was prepared to murder this nigga right where he stood. They placed his head near the water, prepared to drown his ass if necessary. I kneeled down, looking at him with my nostrils flaring.

"You been causing trouble since you got here. I don't know you, nigga, and you don't know me. I should be the only motherfucker in this house talking about setting examples, and you about to be one. Let's get one thing straight here. The next time you put your hands on Rylee or talk to her in a way I don't like, we gone have big fucking problems. If she call me and tell me you fucking with her, I'm gone pay your bitch ass a lil' visit. It seems to me that you can't stay in the same house as everybody and not cause trouble, so I'm gone give you a choice. If you stay here, I'm gone kill you, and the problem is gonna be solved. You leave, you keep your life."

He looked hesitant about whether he wanted to test my gangster or not. Deciding that he wanted to keep his life, he packed his shit and left with a quickness. After all the trouble, I was headed to Rylee's room to check on her, but Remi stopped me before I could get all the way up the steps.

"Trigg, can I talk to you?" she asked.

"Not right now, I'm about to go check on your sister."

"Rylee's fine, trust me."

"What you want, Remi?"

"I wanna thank you for doing what you did."

"I was getting tired of that nigga; he had to go," I shrugged, trying to walk past her, but she grabbed me again.

"That's not the only thing I wanted to say."

"Talk to me," I sighed.

"Trigg, are you gonna be busy later?"

"I don't know, probably not."

"I was thinking about going to the beach later. Do you wanna come?"

"No disrespect, Remi. I see you, baby girl, I really do, but I'm not interested."

"What?"

"I'm not interested. You seem like a cool girl. You pretty as hell, but I don't want you."

"But you want my sister?"

"This ain't about her."

She leaned in and stood on her toes, placing her lips to my ear. Her hand slipped under my Adidas shirt, caressing my chest. She let out a sly moan before breathing on my neck.

"Whatever you think she can do, I can do better. I'd much rather show you what I'm working with than tell you. I can suck you, fuck you, and treat you way better than her. Since the first day I saw you, I wanted you inside me, and I saw how you looked at me. How about we stop playing these games and give each other what we really want?" she whispered in my ear. I licked my lips and pulled her closer, making sure to rest my hand on her lower back. She was so close, I knew she felt my dick pressing up against her.

"You know what I really want?"

"What?" she asked, seductively.

"To fuck your sister until she nut. Nah, I wanna eat her out until she tells me she can't take it anymore. That's what I really want. You have fun at the beach, though," I smiled before walking up the steps. I wasn't about to keep sugarcoating shit with Remi, and one thing was for certain. I was going to tell a motherfucker how I felt. I didn't even care to look at the dumb ass look on her face before going to Rylee's room. When I opened the door, she was sitting on her bed, sketching on a piece of paper. Lloyd's "You" played from her phone as she kept her attention on her paper.

Can I be for real?

Dis is how I feel

I'm in need of love

So let's dip up out of here

Ooohh ya just my type

Everything's so right

I just wanna chill

Let's dip up out of here

She didn't even notice me until I knocked. Looking up at me, she gave me a weak smile before waving me over. Closing the door behind me, I took a seat next to her before looking down at the sketch. Rylee had a hell of a lot of talent because what I was looking at was true art. It was a drawing of the tiger we had seen at the safari the other day.

"Damn, that's nice," I complimented.

"Thanks, I couldn't get her out of my head since we left."

"Sounds like how I'm gone feel after this trip."

"Cree, can we talk?"

"Yeah, what's on your mind, beautiful?"

"This doesn't feel right."

"What doesn't feel right?"

"Us. I mean, I've never in my life talked to anyone younger than me, but all I can think about is this week slowly coming to an end, and I don't want it to. Cree, you've made this trip a lot better than I expected it to be."

"I understand where you're coming from. But you can't spend your entire life worrying about what's going to happen in the future. Let's worry about now, and when that time comes, we can worry about it then."

"I just don't wanna be hurt again. I've been broken before."

"I told you from the jump, I'm a grown ass man. Age ain't got shit to do with anything. If you want me to be real with you, I will. I'm here to break your back, not your heart — if you let me," I said, making her look me in my eyes. I could tell by the way her body shivered that I sent chills down her spine with my statement.

"You can't keep talking like that," she blushed.

"You ain't answer the question."

"I'll think on that," she smiled before pecking my cheek. I sucked my teeth before grabbing her by her neck, giving it a light squeeze.

"You're wrong for that petty ass kiss."

"Then show me how I should've done it," she smiled.

I pressed my lips to hers, making sure to stick my tongue in her mouth. I could taste the Mike and Ike's she was eating not long ago. When we heard the door open, I pulled away to see KC looking at me with a goofy look on her face.

"Oh, was I interrupting something?" she asked.

"Nah, I was just about to head out there," I stood up and walked out. Rylee really had a nigga head fucked up, and I wasn't gonna lie and say I didn't like it.

"You know I can suck a dint out of a car, right?" KC told Porsha, while gripping her ass.

All I could do was shake my head and laugh. I never thought I'd see the day that Porsha's ass got turned out by a woman. She was on KC's ass like a newborn attached to its mama's titty. All they did was say sexual shit to one another and kiss and hug up on each other all day.

"Is she always like this?" I asked Cree as I looked up at him.

We were on our way to Family Kingdom, and it was beautiful out. We had two more days left of this trip, and we decided to explore the rest of what Myrtle Beach had to offer. Ever since Cree got rid of Darnell, the energy in the house had been a lot better, besides Remi's little side eyes and slick comments. Porsha was booed up with KC, and Cree and I were attached at each other's hips. Remi, on the other hand, was annoyed with Bozz and often pushed him away. She pushed him away so much, he ended up meeting some girl, who was walking the strip with her friends and hit it off with her. Now Remi was following behind everyone looking like a lost puppy.

"Yeah, she is," Cree laughed.

"You niggas talking shit? I know you motherfuckers not talking when y'all matching, looking like a whole married couple," KC retorted.

I shook my head before looking down at me and Cree's outfits. I sported a brown Fashion Nova Simplicity long sleeve jumpsuit with a pair of brown Michael Kors Sadler Logo Jacquard Wedge Sandals. My once bone straight bundles were now crimped to perfection, and I accessorized with gold jewelry. Cree had on a pair of brown Playboy sweatpants with the matching sweatshirt, and a pair of brown Retros clung to his feet. We didn't even plan on dressing alike; it just happened, and neither of us decided to go change.

"You niggas mad because y'all ain't match?" Cree flicked KC off.

"How long we finna be out here? I'm already ready to go," Remi complained.

"Yo, what's your problem?" I snapped, already getting tired of her attitude.

"I don't have a problem," Remi rolled her eyes.

"No, apparently you do. You've been giving me the cold shoulder when it should be the other way around. You really about to piss me off."

"Yo, don't let her get to you." Cree grabbed me before I ended up beating her ass.

I wasn't about to spend the duration of my trip going back and forth with Remi. All I knew was that this was going to be a learning experience, and I damn sure wasn't going to invite her to shit else.

"Guys, chill. Everybody, calm down," said the girl Bozz invited.

"Excuse me, what is yo' name?" Porsha asked. I was just as curious.

"My name is Jennifer," she introduced herself.

"But like I was saying, you guys need to calm down. In fact, I got something that can calm everyone down," she said, reaching in her bra.

"Ohhh shit! See, that's what I'm talking about. Jennifer, if you got that gas, I can fuck with you," said KC.

When she pulled out a bag that had a white substance in it, everyone's eyes grew as big as golf balls. She opened it and dumped a little on her hand before sniffing it clean off.

"Bitch, is that crack?" I asked, still astonished.

"Oh my God, Bozz done befriended a fucking crackhead. I thought I seen it all."

"Hey, I mean, I know it's not for everybody. Here, I got something else," Jennifer said, reaching behind her ear and passing Bozz a blunt. Bozz passed it to KC, and KC threw it in Jennifer's face.

"Is there meth in that blunt?!" KC yelled. "This bitch tryna give us meth," she shook her head.

"Jesus Devonte Christ, I'm done. I just wanna know, is you or is you not a crackhead? Because bitch, that looks like crack," said Porsha.

"Y'all talking about crack; I'm still on the meth in the blunt," said Bozz.

"Uh uh, sweetheart you gotta go. We don't do those things over here," said Bozz.

She tried to explain herself, but she walked off, still snorting her coke.

"Bozz invited a damn crackhead. I really can't believe this shit," KC laughed, shaking her head.

"The bitch was gone buy me some food," he shrugged.

We all shared a laugh before finally walking into Family Kingdom. After we bought a bunch of tickets, everyone went their separate ways. Cree and I went on multiple rides, from the sling shot, roller coasters, and even bumper cars. He'd even won me two big ass, life size teddy bears. We walked around the park, holding hands, getting to know each other more.

"You having fun?" he asked.

"You know I am," I smiled.

"You hungry?"

"I can eat."

The entire walk to Friendly's, all I could do was laugh at the jokes he told. Being around Cree made me feel a feeling that I hadn't felt in years. The way he held conversations with me, the way he held me, kissed me, it all gave me such a euphoric feeling. I stared into his eyes as we sat in the booth across from one another, sharing a basket of fries. Friendly's definitely gave that old 90's diner vibe, and I was feeling it.

Ever since you crossed my path

Everything is different

You always know just how to make me laugh

You got me all up in my feelings

And as much as I love the feeling

I hate it, it gets me frustrated

Wanna say just how I feel

"And I just wanna hold you all night long. Whenever I'm around you, nothing's wrong," I sang and bobbed my head to Queen Naija's "Butterflies". When he started staring at me, I hid my face, only for him to reach across the table and pull my hands down.

"Stop hiding that beautiful ass smile from me."

"I'm not hiding anything," I blushed.

"Yes, you do. Every time I make you smile or laugh, you act shy."

"Because of how you look at me."

"How do I look at you?"

"You know how you look at me," I shook my head.

"I can't help it. When I want something, I can't help but to stare."

"Mhm, whatever. Probably use that line on them girls back in your hometown."

"Nah, I don't. I'm not usually this friendly. You just caught my eye, and I can't help but to keep you in my presence."

"To think, I thought you were cocky and self-centered when I first met you."

"I thought you were uptight and still do," he laughed.

"Damn, I knew you were an asshole. But I'm fine with that."

"I bet you are. You seem like the type of woman who loves when a man takes charge."

"I do."

"That explains a lot."

"What do you mean?"

"I just got that vibe from you."

"And do you prefer to be submissive or dominant?"

"I prefer to be dominant, but I'm submissive to the right woman."

As soon as my phone started to die, Cree and I decided to go back to the house. When we got there, the house was quiet. From the looks of it, everyone was still out and about. Going upstairs, I kicked off my shoes and placed my two teddy bears to the side. Sitting on the edge of my bed, I sighed, debating on if I wanted to go through with what was on my mind. All I kept hearing was Porsha's loud ass in my head, telling me to fuck this man. Even with her not being in the house right now, I already knew how shit would've been if she was sitting right in front of me. Shit, she was making the best of being here by letting KC lick her ass up and down like a lollipop. I was always nervous when it came to stepping outside of the box and taking risks, and right now was one of those moments.

"Fuck it, nope, can't do it," I said to myself.

I closed my room door before stripping out of my jumpsuit, leaving me in only my red lace lingerie set. Turning on my TV, I went to Spotify and clicked the first playlist on my list. The sound of knocking on my door caught my attention.

"Who is it?"

"Cree."

"Shit," I mumbled, looking around frantically for something to cover myself up with. Not being able to find anything, I walked over to the door, opening it halfway and peeking my head out.

"Wassup?"

"You going to sleep anytime soon?" he asked.

"No, why?"

"KC and your girl, Porsha, went out to this strip club, and Bozz still got your sister occupied at Family Kingdom. Was thinking about chillin' in the living room and watching a movie. But from the looks of it, you about to jump in bed," he said, looking through the cracks.

"Oh no, I can come out and watch a movie with you, no problem," I smiled, closing the door a little more to hide my body.

"Why you doing that?" he quizzed, stroking his beard.

"Doing what?"

"First, you hide that beautiful smile; now, you hiding that sexy ass body."

"Trust me, hiding my body is a good thing. You and your hormones been raging lately."

"What you tryna say?"

"I'm trying to say I'm too much for you."

"That's why you don't wanna go there with me? You think I can't handle it?"

"Cree, sweetheart, I'm too much woman for you."

As if that was permission, he opened my door fully before his eyes roamed from my face all the way down to my feet. The way he licked his lips and the glisten in his eye always seemed to drive me crazy, and I had to control myself every time. Every step he took forward, I stepped back. He closed the door with his foot before coming closer, towering over me.

"Maybe I'm too much man for you, and that's the real reason

you so nervous around me."

"I—"

"I'm not gonna go back and forth with you about which one of us is the most dominant. I'd rather show you," he interrupted me, before pulling his sweatshirt from over his head, revealing his bare chest. My kitty quivered through my lace Vickies. I couldn't help but to place my hand below his belly button and slide it all the way up to his pecs, where there was a tattoo of a ship in an ocean with Matthew 8:23 under it. I was so mesmerized by all the ink on his body.

"I'm a man who likes to ask for permission. But I also like when a woman tells me everything she wants me to do to her," he lifted my chin up, making me look at him.

"You know what I want you to do to me."

"I wanna hear you say it."

"Cree, I—"

"Say it," he repeated himself, this time pulling me closer and gripping my ass. I could feel my lips spread just from the way he gripped it.

"I want you to fuck me," I said, barely above a whisper.

He picked my ass up swiftly as if I was nothing. His knees didn't buckle, he didn't sound out of breath, and his ass didn't even break a sweat. He walked me over to the bed, laying me down gently, making sure to spread my legs.

Let's talk about my sex drive

And how you look so good just sitting by my left side

And how I just got wet

Let's fuck in the whip real quick

I know we got somewhere to get

I don't care if it get too lit

I don't know if I'm wildin'

Tiara Thomas's song, "Sex Drive", played from the TV as Cree kissed in between my thighs. Just from the way his hands caressed my body, I knew that he was trying to handle me with care. My breath hitched when I felt him slide my panties to the side. He trailed his tongue from my inner thighs all the way to my second set of lips. His thumb brushed down my slit, causing a shiver to run down my spine. As soon as his mouth attached to my clit, I let out a light gasp. He was doing so many tricks with his tongue, I couldn't keep my composure. All I could do was grip the sheets and arch my back in pleasure. I was so wet, I knew for a fact his beard was going to be soaked. A mixture of my juices and his spit slid down to the crack of my ass. He slipped his finger into my pussy, all while giving my clit the most attention. I ran my fingers through his waves before pushing his head deeper. Just hearing him moan and slurp on my clit drove my body crazy. My body shook as I came over his face.

He stood up slowly, staring at me. His beard was now coated in my juices, and his lips glistened like diamonds in the sun. My chest heaved up and down as my legs shook. I'd never received head that had my body react in such a way. His tongue traced over his thick, pink lips before he dropped his sweats, revealing his dick. He brought big dick energy to the table, and he was definitely packing something serious. My eyes admired how blessed he was. He had girth and length, and the way it stood at attention gave me clarification that he was going to send me out of this room limping. He placed the tip at my entrance before staring at me with those same lust-filled eyes. My kitty quivered more when he placed his hands at my throat.

"How bad do you want it?" His voice was smooth as butter yet deeper than the ocean.

"Stop teasing me."

"I'd rather tease you 'cause if I give you all of it, I'm gone have your ass in here crying."

"Back that shit up, then," I egged him on. He kneeled down in my face and pecked my lips before damn near ripping my bra from my body, revealing my double D breasts.

"I'm gonna only tell you this once and one time only. No matter how many times you cum, how much you squirt, how hard your legs shake, or if you scream so much, you no longer have a voice until the next day, I'm not stopping until I knock your beautiful ass off that high horse. Like I told you before, I'm here to break your back, not your heart. You ready for that?"

"Yes," I replied. I felt so weak with just how shaky my response came out.

He slid in, making sure to spread my legs even more to give himself more room. Hearing him hiss while sliding in, I gripped the sheets and let out a sly moan.

S-T-R-O-K-E

I need that stroke

Oh, give me that S-T-R-O-K-E

Fiendin' that stroke

Just lay me on my back

And make me curl my toes

When I get that stroke

And every time I'm mad

You know just what I want

I want that stroke (stroke)

This boy had to have been a pornstar on the low. My ass was up in here with lockjaw because of how he was giving me long, deep strokes, His strokes matched the beat of the music, only turning me on more. I felt like this nigga was touching my soul just from the way he sucked and kissed on my neck, all while pumping in and out of me.

"Fuck! Cree."

"You like that?" he groaned in my ear.

"Yes!" I moaned as I gripped his ass. As soon as he started to pick up the pace, my eyes damn near rolled to the back of my bed. I felt my walls tightening around his dick, and before I knew it, I was cumming. I couldn't even catch my breath or get myself together because he was still going in.

"Cree!" I screamed his name. I was on the brink of cumming yet again.

"That's it, cum for me. Cum on this dick."

I gasped before digging my nails into his back, for sure knowing I was going to draw blood. He was putting my poor lil' pussy through it, and I was regretting ever testing him.

"You so fucking wet. I'm trying to not give your ass a baby." He pulled out and stood back, staring at me with hooded eyes.

"Turn around."

"Cree, I'm tired. I can't."

"Either you turn around or I'm gone turn you around," he stated. I could see my nut dripping off the tip of his dick and his veins pulsating. He was definitely hung like a horse, and he was backing up everything he said.

"Cree, please. Give me like five minutes," I said out of breath. He walked up and dragged me to the edge of the bed, flipping my ass like a pancake. I yelped out as his palm landed a firm slap on my ass.

"Bend over and spread your cheeks," he commanded.

I did as told, and he instantly slid in from the back, making sure to put his thumb in my ass. I gripped the sheets as he pounded me from the back. We were going at it for a good minute, and I felt like I needed an oxygen machine.

"You had enough?" he asked.

"Mhm," I mumbled, still on all fours with my face mashed into the pillow. My eyes were heavy, and all I wanted to do was go to sleep. Cree walked out of the room before coming back in and cleaning me up then tucking me in. This nigga really fucked me good and then had the nerve to put me to sleep like a baby. What the hell did I get myself into with this man?

"Promise to send me pictures of that pussy, every day," KC's dramatic ass fake cried to Porsha.

Today was officially our last day in Myrtle Beach, and when I say a nigga was dreading it, I was dreading it. After finally getting that moment with Rylee, I felt like shit was just getting started for us. I knew this day was coming, and so did she. We had given Janet back the keys to the house, and everyone was saying their final goodbyes. Leaning on the car with my arms crossed, I watched as Rylee approached me. Just knowing that we were about to go our separates ways almost made a nigga shed some tears.

"Hey," she greeted. I could see the sadness in her eyes as clear as day.

"What's good?"

"Don't do that," she pouted.

"Do what?"

"Go back to that thug ass bad boy shit you were doing when I first met you. Come on, Cree."

"You tryna read me, Ms. Artello?'"

"I don't know, Mr. Wright, am I?" she smiled.

"Give me a hug. I'm gonna miss your crazy ass," I smiled.

She walked into my arms, trying to give me a funky ass hug until I sucked my teeth at her, making her laugh. She wrapped her arms around me as I inhaled the scent of her sweet perfume that instantly made a nigga go on rock. I shook my head and laughed to myself when I saw Remi giving me the side eye.

"I think your sister's mad at us."

"Let's give her a reason to be mad," she smiled before cupping my face and giving me a nice big kiss. Remi sucked her teeth before walking off towards the car.

"You gone stay in touch?" I asked.

"You know I am."

"I don't know; I'm just trusting your word."

"Well, you can trust me."

"Come on, Rylee, it's hot, and I'm ready to go!" Remi yelled out the window of her car.

"I gotta go. But before I do, I wanna thank you."

"Thank me for what?"

"For making this trip memorable for me."

"I should be thanking you for that. Give me your phone."

She reached into her back pocket and pulled out her phone before handing it to me. After spending a week with her, it didn't even dawn on me that we hadn't even exchanged numbers. Saving my number in her phone, I pecked her forehead, feeling my heart shatter.

"Hit me up as soon as you touch down."

"I will," she smiled.

I watched her walk away, still trying to accept the fact that she was leaving. Cranking my car up, I looked in the backseat to see Bozz already knocked out. Rylee had cooked a big ass breakfast for everyone this morning, and I already knew that once Bozz ate some good ass food, he was gonna be out for a minute. I looked over at KC, who had her tongue down Porsha's throat. They acted like they weren't fucking the entire week here, but I understood completely. We got used to being around them for an entire week, and now that it was time to go back to our regular lives, it was hard. I watched as KC smacked Porsha's ass while she walked back to her car. KC jumped into the passenger's seat before I pulled off and headed back home.

"I want my money from both of you bitch ass niggas," said KC.

"I ain't got no problem giving you your funky ass money."

"Yeah, it's funky when you lose. But I ain't even finna cap, I'm gonna miss my lil' freak for the week," she pouted.

"You got her number?"

"Hell yeah, I got her number. Just know next year, nigga, we going New Orleans. It don't even gotta be next year. Nigga, we going this summer."

"Nah, I know for a fact I got shit going on with Red Haven this summer. But for Spring Break next year, I know for a fact that I'll be down for that."

"Aight, bet. When was the last time you talked to your mom?" she asked.

"I only talked to her four times since I've been here. I guess I was so occupied, I forgot," I sighed. That shit sounded bad.

"I'm pretty sure she's straight. And if anything would have gone down, my mom would have called us. You know that," she nudged my shoulder.

"I know."

> *Had to remind myself, had to re-find myself*
>
> *How to refine myself, how to define myself*

How to resign myself, how to rely on myself

Got a lot of shit I don't even want

I'm sendin' everything back though

All the energy I don't even want

I'm sendin' everything back though

Even though I brought it on myself

I'm sendin' everything back though

"Patience" by Russ played through my car as the sound of the rain hit the roof of my car. The weather was nice and sunny the entire week here, so I was happy we didn't get stuck with rain. For the entire drive back home, all I could do was think about Rylee. The night I explored every inch of her body, the sweet sound of her euphoric moans, the way her nails pierced through my skin, the sweet taste of her nectar, the way she looked at me, asking for persimmon to cum, was all surreal. I'd never fucked a woman as good as I laid down pipe with Rylee.

"Nigga, what you thinking about? You real quiet," KC quizzed.

"I ain't thinking about shit," I shrugged.

"Nigga, we grew up together. I know when something is on your mind. Is it about your mom? Talk to me."

"It's Rylee."

"Oh shit, she done put that seasoned pussy on ya. I knew you beat the pussy up good 'cause your ass been smiling big as hell since the other night."

"I did," I chuckled, shaking my head.

"What's the problem, though?"

"Leaving just don't feel right."

"You gone miss her thick ass?"

"Don't make me sound like a punk ass nigga 'cause you know I'm far from it."

"Ain't nothing wrong with being an emotional gangster. If you miss shawty, just say that. I miss my lil' Nola baby already. I don't think I'll ever find a bitch in Charlotte who speaks Creole while I'm eating the pussy."

"I'm gonna miss her, I ain't finna lie to you."

"Hey, at least your girl from South Carolina; mine is Louisiana. Charleston is what? Three hours away from home."

"She's not my girl."

"You want her to be, though."

"Worry about yourself," I shrugged her off.

When we touched down in North Carolina, I could already feel the stress placed back on my shoulders. On the way here, KC had received a call about some new lil' niggas fucking things up, giving Red Haven a bad look. I hadn't even been home long before I had to come back, fucking lil' niggas up.

"Y'all want me to drop you off at home, or you chillin' at my spot?" I asked.

"Your spot," said Bozz.

"Same," added KC.

The sound of sirens alerted my ears from behind. I stopped my car like the others to let the emergency vehicles pass by. KC, Bozz, and I looked at each other when we noticed that they were going into my neighborhood. I slammed my foot on the gas, driving like a bat out of hell towards my house. When I pulled up, the ambulance was already parked on the curb and rushing inside of my mother's house. KC, Bozz, and I jumped out of the car before running inside. My heart was on the fucking ground because I was praying they weren't here for what I thought they were here for. KC's mom came out of the house with tears in her eyes.

"Cree, baby, I'm so sorry," she cried, reaching out to me, but I stepped back.

"What are you talking about?"

"I stayed the night with her because she said she wasn't feeling well. When she woke up, I cooked for her, we watched some TV, and talked. Then, she took a nap, and I checked for her pulse and…and…an—" She broke down in KC's arms before I ran in with Bozz on my trail. When I saw them putting her on the gurney and pulling a white sheet over her face, I tried to run to her, but Bozz pulled me back. I was screaming and crying like a fucking baby.

"No! That's my fucking mama! Y'all could have saved her!" I cried.

I dropped to my knees, feeling like I was about to pass out. My soul felt as if it had left from my body. I couldn't breathe; my mother was gone. I wasn't going to be the same after this shit, and I didn't even know how I was going to go on.

"And done," I smiled, looking around my new apartment. I had been in Georgia for a week, and just like that, my entire apartment was finished. I was thankful that I ordered my furniture ahead of time. All I really had to do was decorate, and I loved everything I did to my apartment. I was so busy trying to get settled in, I hadn't had time to do much of anything. My first day of class started tomorrow, and I was super excited. I took a seat on my ash gray couch before pulling my new phone from my pocket. Just looking at my brand new phone still pissed me off because I missed my old one. On the way back from Myrtle Beach, Remi, Porsha, and I had one hell of a drive back, and I was surprised we made it back home in one piece. Porsha had finally told me the true reason she beat Remi's ass the way she did. After hearing that,

I wanted to slam on brakes and beat her ass myself. Purposely inviting Darnell was grimy, and I would never forgive her for that.

Then, what made shit worse was that she fucked him a few weeks after we ended things. I knew Remi was sneaky, but her being sneaky with me really hurt. I loved my sister, and I'd do anything for her, but after all of that, I don't think I could find it in me to forgive her. Just hearing that she was in Georgia because she was attending the school I was teaching at still didn't sit right with me. I was praying that her ass wasn't in any of my classes because I was prepared to fail her ass just for being a nuisance. Even after the multiple talks with my parents about making things right with her, I still wasn't budging. What pissed me off the most was that she was truly upset that Cree and I were talking. She ended up throwing my phone out on the freeway, and we almost got into an accident because Porsha was fucking her ass up in the backseat. The whole situation was messy and annoying, and I was glad it was finally over.

What made me even more pissed was that I didn't even get a chance to back up my phone before she tossed it, so I no longer had Cree's number. I didn't want him to think I was intentionally ignoring him. I found myself casually stalking his Instagram, debating on hitting him up on there, but I assumed he was upset with me. I beat myself up every day in my apartment about it, but then I came to the realization that what went down during Spring Break was just temporary. I was a professor now, and I was no longer in South Carolina. I couldn't live my life as if I was still in my early twenties. Cree made my experience a lot better, and I thanked him heavily for that, but the real world was dragging me back to reality, and that was where I needed to be. Standing up, I walked over to my mirror, admiring myself. My hair was braided neatly in box braids, and I sported a pair of green cargo jeans, a plaid shirt that I wore open, and a pair of white foam Yeezy's.

I'd finally had the time to meet with Drayton, and I was excited. After texting for months, we were finally able to meet each other. I applied lip gloss to my lips before grabbing my keys and heading towards my car. "Can't Be Friends" by Trey Songz played through my car as I drove towards Carrabba's Italian Grill. Finding a parking spot, I got out of the car and went inside. When I saw Drayton across the room, sipping out of a mug, I walked over. I guess he felt my presence because he looked up at me. He had a big smile across his face. His six-foot four frame and muscular body were definitely more defined in person than over FaceTime calls.

"Well, if it isn't Ms. Artello. The beautiful woman I've been dying to meet for quite some time now."

"Drayton, it's nice to finally see you in person," I smiled.

"Likewise. My apologies about when you first arrived. I wanted to meet with you then, but I had a family emergency."

"Is everything okay?" I asked.

"Uh, not really." He pulled my chair out for me as I took a seat. He then took his seat right across from me.

"What's going on? If you don't mind me asking."

"I don't wanna bother you with my problems."

"Oh, you're not bothering me."

"It's my ex-wife; she passed away."

"Oh my God, I'm sorry to hear that. How are you holding up?"

"Taking it one day at a time. I knew it was coming; the entire family knew."

"If you ever wanna talk about it, I'm here." I reached my hand across the table and rested it on top of his.

"I'll keep that in mind. So, how are you liking it here?"

"Uh, it's definitely different from back home."

"I hope that's different in a good way," he chuckled, toying with his salt and pepper beard.

"Yes, it is. I'm still getting used to everything."

"Are you ready to teach your first class tomorrow?"

"I am, I'm a little nervous."

"Trust me, teaching adults is a lot better than teaching middle schoolers."

"I hope so. I miss my middle schoolers already, though," I smiled weakly.

"I bet you do. I know how it feels to bond with students and then have to leave. I was actually a professor before I became a dean. I watched so many students walk across that stage. It's definitely an experience."

"Well, tell me more."

Drayton and I talked about everything that could come to our minds. For him to be forty-two, he sure wore it well. He held a good conversation, just how he did during texts, and he made sure to keep a smile on my face. The entire day consisted of Drayton and I exploring parts of the city. He kept his word about being my tour guide, and I truly enjoyed it. When I got back into my house, I found myself wrapped up in bed watching, Baby Boy, snuggled up with the big ass teddy bears Cree had won me. I could still smell his Versace Eros cologne on them. Getting out of bed, I went to my closet and pulled out a box of things I had purchased from Myrtle Beach. The box contained T-shirts I had purchased, along with a few more souvenirs. I came across the photos of Cree and I at the Safari Tour. Picking it up, I smiled weakly, brushing my thumb across it. Just seeing the happy look on my face when I was around him couldn't compare to anything in this world. Whoever captured this photo definitely caught a Kodak moment. I could hear the photo in my head. Just hearing Cree be a big ass baby about not wanting to get into the water because he thought the tiger was going to bite him, was still quite humorous to me.

I missed him like crazy but I knew I couldn't spend my time reminiscing how I wanted to.

"I'm sorry," I said, kissing the picture before placing it back into the box and putting it back in the corner of my closet.

Cree "Trigg" Wright

I can't lie I wanted you, the first time that I saw you

Tried to diss me till, you realized I'm someone

You could talk to, You've been hurt over and over, tell me

What has it taught you, Soon as you fell for me

Tho I had caught you, dead your exes

Don't let them haunt you

"You've been quiet lately. You okay?" asked my dad.

I'd just gotten in the car, and he hadn't even given me a whole five minutes of silence before throwing questions at me. A nigga was feeling homesick already, and I didn't even wanna be here. After my mom had passed, I'd taken that shit harder than anyone else. I hadn't eaten or even slept until after her funeral. I came across her will, and everything my dad told me was in it. Moving to Georgia and going back to college wasn't something I imagined myself doing, but I did it. After my mom's funeral, I hopped in my car and drove straight here to see that my dad had already thought ahead. I had my own spot, and he had me already enrolled in school. Even though enrollment was late, he got away with that shit because he was the dean. Today was my first day of class, and to be honest, I wanted to drop out already. I was still grieving and wanted to be alone. KC and Bozz still kept in touch. If it wasn't for me having so much trust in them to run Red Haven without me, I would have never come.

"I'm straight," I shrugged.

"I know you, Creshawn; you're not straight. You're my son. I know when something is on your mind."

"I'm just tryna get used to being down here."

"I know it's a big adjustment. Your mom would be proud of —"

"Don't tell me what she would be proud of. I don't wanna talk about her right now."

"We don't have to talk about her; we can talk about something else."

"Like?"

"Like your trip to Myrtle Beach, how was it? Did you enjoy yourself?"

"It was aight."

Just hearing about Myrtle Beach pissed me off. I had a hell of a good time; I truly did, but after coming home to my mom no longer being on this earth, I blamed myself. Something told me not to leave, but I did. I should have checked on her more, I should have left early and came home to her. I should have fucking stayed. Then, to make shit worse, I made the biggest fucking mistake of my life trusting a bitch I only knew for a week. When my mom died, I wanted Rylee to be that shoulder I cried on. I wanted her to be there for me like she said she was going to be. A nigga had been waiting on her call for the longest and never got it. That shit turned me cold, and no bitch on this earth would ever get that side of me again.

"Met anybody?" my dad asked.

"Nah, didn't go up there planning to meet anybody."

"Can I tell you something, son?"

"Wassup?"

"I'm talking to somebody new."

"Does she know she's gonna be ex-wife number three? Looks like Cassidy hit the road."

"You tryna be funny?"

"I'm just stating a fact."

"Listen, she's different."

"How's she different from the last one?"

"She's younger, beautiful, and she's w—"

"You dating younger women now? Pops, somebody's gonna use your ass for all your money. Watch out with that."

"She's not like that."

"When I'm gone meet her?"

"You might meet her today. She's actually a new professor here."

"She is?"

"Yeah."

"You should know better than mixing business and pleasure."

"Am I the father, or are you?"

"I'm just stating a fact," I laughed lightly.

"Yeah, stating a fact, my ass."

He pulled into his parking spot before the both of us got out of the car. Walking inside, I caught a glimpse of my fit, and from the way the bitches were already eyeing a nigga down, I knew I had it in the bag. I sported a white tee, light brown RockStar

Original sweats, a pair of white Forces, and my Nike backpack hung off my shoulder.

"Don't get yourself in trouble here, son," said my dad, giving me the side eye.

"What you mean?"

"The women up here in Georgia are different. Don't let these chicken head lil' girls knock you off the real reason you're here."

"I got me."

"I hope so."

I followed him to his office while he tried to get my schedule printed out. I took a seat in front of his desk before pulling my phone out. Scrolling through Instagram, a certain someone's post caught my attention. I hadn't even noticed that I followed Remi back on the gram. She was posed up in front of the same building I was in. Her caption read, Mommiana's about to cop this degree. I shook my head and laughed lightly. It was a small ass world. I would be lying if I said she didn't look good as hell in this picture. She sported some black leggings, Michael Kors sandals, and a University of Georgia shirt that she had tide in a knot so you'd be able to see her belly button piercing. Clicking her name, I decided to do something she had been wanting me to do for the longest.

TrillyTriggRH: What's good witchu

RemiRabbit: Nothing much, what you up to?

TrillyTriggRH: That's what I'm tryna figure out witchu. I see we in the same building.

"Here you go, son," my dad interrupted my conversation. He handed me my schedule, along with a map of the school. I stood up to walk out and meet Remi's ass for some top until the door opened. When it opened, I damn near broke my neck, seeing Rylee standing there. She sported a black blouse with black and white striped slacks. Her hair was pulled back, giving me a view of her beautiful features. All we could do was lock eyes with each other, not even knowing what to say. All I knew, was that her ass owed me an explanation.

"Ah, son, here's the wonderful lady. This right here is Ms. Artello. She's actually one of your professors. And the woman I was telling you about in the car," he smiled. All I could do was look at her with wide eyes, and I chuckled to myself.

"You had one thing right about her, she is beautiful," I nodded my head. All she could do was stand there, looking nervous and stupid.

"Ms. Artello, this is my son, Creshawn," he introduced us. I was about to rain on her entire fucking parade. All I could think about was her fucking my dad being the reason she curved a nigga.

"We actually kn—"

"Nice to meet you, Creshawn," she interrupted me. She extended her hand out for me to shake it. Was this really the game she wanted to play?

"Likewise," I replied, shaking her hand. I could still smell her sweet perfume, reminiscing of the night I explored her body. The way my nose nuzzled into her neck, inhaling her essence.

My father's phone began to ring. He quickly picked it up before giving the person on the other end of the line an aggravated tone.

"I gotta go down the hall real fast; I'll be right back," he told the both of us. As soon as he left the room, I looked at Rylee with a look that could kill.

"Cree, I'm sorr—."

"It's Trigg or Mr. Wright to you," I stopped her.

"Are we really doing this right now?"

"We are and you know we are."

"To think I was really feeling you. I thought after what we did, you were feeling me too, but I guess not."

"Don't do that."

"Don't do what? Tell you the truth? Rylee, you fucking lied to me, and that shit hurt. When I left that day, I came back home, and my mama was fucking dead. I needed you."

"I'm sorr—"

"Fuck your sorry. Do you know how many fucking times I stood by my fucking phone waiting for that shit to ring? How many nights I stayed up, thinking about your ass?! You're fucking selfish, and I regret ever trusting you." I had to calm myself down because I felt myself getting angry just thinking about that shit. She looked as if she was about to cry, but I could give a rat's ass about that shit. She grabbed me by my shirt and pulled me in, pressing her lips to mine. She then pulled away, shaking her head at me.

"Don't ever call me selfish. I ended up losing my phone that day, and it wasn't backed up. I couldn't get in touch with you. I found you on Instagram a few days later, but I was scared. I was scared that if I reached out to you, you would react just like this. Cree, I would never hurt you, ever. I want you to believe that."

Staring at her, I truly wanted to believe her, but I couldn't — especially now that we were in this situation. She was fucking on my pops, and I just couldn't look at her the same.

"What about him?" I asked, referring to my dad.

"What about him?

"You fucking him?"

"Cree, no. Drayton and I just talk. That's it, that's all, we just talk."

"So, what now? You want me to stand back and watch you

cake it up with my pops and be my teacher? Act like shit is normal? What do you want me from me, Rylee?"

"Remember what you told me back in Myrtle Beach?"

"I said a lot." She grabbed my hand and made me place them on her throat.

"Ask me."

"Rylee—"

"I said, ask me."

"How bad do you want it?"

"Bad enough to break every rule to have you," she stared into my eyes. This girl really had me wrapped around her finger, and all I could do was stand there. She wanted to play a risky game, and that was what I was going to give her. I removed my hands from her throat the second my dad walked back inside the office.

"My apologies about that. I had an issue I had to resolve. So, are you guys ready for this semester?"

Rylee and I looked at each other before sharing a smile we knew too often.

"Oh, we're ready," I smirked.

THE END

**WANT TO INTERACT WITH T'ANN MARIE & HER TEAM?
JOIN OUR READERS GROUP ON FACEBOOK!**

https://bit.ly/2TfYBL

WIN PRIZES, BE APART OF LIVE BOOK DISCUSSIONS & MORE!

Join Our Mailing List

http://eepurl.com/gU81k5

TMP
TANN MARIE PRESENTS
is now accepting submissions in the following genres

URBAN FICTION * URBAN ROMANCE
STREET LIT * URBAN PARANORMAL
INTERRACIAL ROMANCE

for consideration, please email the first 5 chapters of your manuscript to:

TANNMARIESUBS@GMAIL.COM

www.ingramcontent.com/pod-product-compliance
Lightning Source LLC
Chambersburg PA
CBHW071921120726
48001CB00005B/1821